RISING TIDES

WINGS OF ARTEMIS #10

REBECCA ROYCE

Rising Tides (Wings of Artemis #10)

Copyright @ 2019 by Rebecca Royce

Ebook ISBN: 978-1-947672-79-6

Print ISBN: 978-1-947672-80-2

Cover art by Original Syn

Content Editing: Heather Long

Copy/Proofread Editing: Jennifer Jones at Bookends Editing

Formatting: Ripley Proserpina

Published by Rebecca Royce

www.rebeccaroyce.com

 Created with Vellum

Dearest Reader,

Thank you for taking this journey with Amber and me through the galaxy. This is book ten in the Wings of Artemis world and it takes us much closer toward the end of these stories. After this book, there will be two more for a total of twelve. I think you can probably guess at this point who our final heroine will be.

Amber is a character very dear to me, and she has some pretty serious things to face in this book. When I'm writing, I frequently think of books as things other than their titles. Rising Tides to me became The Battle For Earth. It is more than that. It is the battle for who Amber is, who she wants to be, and what happens to her now that she is back where she never wanted to be again.

Amber's story is a second chance at love.

Thank you for taking these trips through space and time with me,

RR

GETTING KNOCKED OVER REALLY SUCKED. But given that I had no choice, I pulled myself to my feet and let the dizziness of the last moment pass before I continued on my way. Brushing the dust off my arms, I trudged forward. The last bombing strafe had come way too close. Evander had started to make a real dent in our external shield barriers, and I wore the dust from the last near miss to prove it. I wiped myself again.

It was my first day as an official doctor and nerves left me practically petrified. I'd almost not hit the dirt in time to avoid getting hit by debris.

"Doctor Chen." Brenden, the Z Warrior assigned to me rushed to my side. "That was close. Are you okay?"

I shrugged even though I didn't feel calm. There were eyes on me all the time. I needed to do a good job of keeping everyone calm. They looked to me for assurance. "Only my ego is bruised."

He cleared his throat, which I learned over the last five months meant he didn't believe me but wouldn't dare to speak his disagreement.

I sighed. "Okay, my shoulder is kind of bruised, too." And probably my behind, but I wasn't going that far as to tell him that part.

The Chen Empire was under constant attack. With no end in sight, we were going to have to figure ways to protect ourselves better. I pointed toward the medical facility. It looked like a small group of abandoned houses. We liked it that way, kept the Evander spaceships from targeting us. I hoped the steps the Super Soldiers had taken to disguise it from Evander scans before they left to go fight continued to hold up.

"I have to go. Waverly is in labor."

"Oh." My Z motioned me onward. He was coming with me. There was no way I'd get a break from one of them following me around today after my near miss. There were fifteen Z Warriors left on the Chen compound with the rest off fighting. Those who remained all seemed to be determined to make sure I stayed alive.

"Brenden, after you deliver me to the medical facility, I need you to go see if you can find Dr. Ari Bennett. I'll be fine inside. I won't go anywhere. But I know he went underground to work with the hidden resistance and help with their injured. This is his wife. He needs to try to get here."

My Z warrior nodded once. "I'll see what I can do. It can be hard in the tunnels, but I'll try to find him."

If anyone could, it was Brenden. The young Z warrior had proved over these months a good friend to me. He'd almost convinced me I could have the Z around and not want to escape or suffer violent anxiety. *Almost.* I was sold on Brenden, just not the whole group.

Waverly's whimper greeted me as I entered the facility. She must have advanced quickly. I'd only received word she was in labor a few minutes earlier. Maybe she hadn't come in quickly. She was a nurse, and she'd been nothing but busy since the fight began.

I rushed to her. "Well, I might not be your first choice doctor. I think that blond husband of yours would fit that bill, but I'll try to be a good number two."

She laughed, which was a good sign. "I thought maybe I could just do it. Women have babies all the time. You didn't need to... Oh," she cried out in pain. "Waste time and resources on me."

I rubbed her shoulder as I studied the machine's read out. I'd love to get her off planet to have this baby, to put her on a spaceship going someplace like Venus, and give her some semblance of safety to give birth, but it was way too late for that now.

"Don't be silly. This is where you belong, always."

Hers was not going to be the first baby I'd delivered. War didn't stop women having babies. It just made it more complicated to keep them all safe after.

I took off my coat and set it aside. I needed to clean up and then offer her what relief I could. "So talking to you is different than talking to someone who isn't in this with us. Should I give you the speech?"

Waverly laughed, it was a good sound. I looked up at her scans. Mother and baby were holding on just fine. She'd had her first child, Emerson, her son with her husband Rohan, not so long ago. There was every reason to believe that this was going to go just fine. Although every pregnancy was different. I washed my hands in hot water, staring at the tap.

The water. In the Chen Empire it was all about the water. Every day I was here taught me more and more what being guardians of the water meant to the people. When I'd lived here the first time I'd given it no thought, but now evidence of their care for it was everywhere, like my eyes were new, seeing everything differently.

"Maybe if we'd spent more time as a society." She groaned, a long sound. "Seeing to the needs of women instead of bartering us off like chattel we'd have an easier time giving birth."

Our methods for childbirth weren't better than they were before the bombs. On the rural planets, what few women there were regularly died in the act. But Waverly would be fine because she had me here.

I touched her arm. "I think there are a lot of things we could have done differently."

She smiled at me. "Maybe it's starting. Maybe you being a full-fledged doctor now is just the start of how things can change."

I pulled her into a hug. Pregnant women needed lots of touch. Waverly didn't have the father of her baby here. He was off fighting a war for all of us. Her one husband remaining was underground helping a resistance. She just had me. And I would not let her down.

"I'm going to take really good care of you. You're not alone. I'm here. Now, let's check you guys out and see what we can do to relieve some of your pain. If we need to, I'll knock you out, deliver the little guy, and heal you up in the machine. Hopefully, we won't need to do it."

She nodded, wiping tears from her eyes. "This will end, right?"

"Yes, I mean, it's hard to tell from the scans, but I'd say we're just hours from seeing your son..."

She shook her head. "Good to know, but no. I mean, the war? It'll end. Jackson, Canyon, Rohan, they'll come home. Ari won't have to keep leaving. Evander will go. We'll all get to go home, right?"

"Absolutely." I nodded my head. "One hundred percent right. They're all coming back."

I hadn't seen my husbands since they'd left. Not one single moment with them. The others had moments. Jackson had come through two months ago on a ship that needed to be repaired. Canyon and Rohan were on a shuttle of Super Soldiers who came for supplies. Waverly saw Ari several times a week.

My sister's husbands had each flown through once so far. Diana's Lewis came through a lot. He wasn't far. There were shelter points all over Earth and Lewis was close. He treated patients and sent them here once they were stable. He was here every few weeks. Sterling had come with Rohan and Canyon. Cash had only left recently on a shuttle. And Damian had made it home twice.

Melissa wasn't here, she was off fighting. Some of their kids were here with Diana and they all came through.

I didn't mean to be jealous, I didn't like the part of me harboring those thoughts, but I was the only one I knew who hadn't had one moment with her husbands since they'd left. Not one word in five months, not one glimpse of them.

With Evander jamming all the signals here, I hadn't even heard their voices.

I smiled at Waverly. I was still so good at faking it and no one required a good dose of calm and happy more than a woman about to give birth. "Let's meet your son today, shall we? And then when Jackson, Rohan, and Canyon come back, and Ari gets up from the tunnels, they'll be so proud of how brave you were."

She smiled at me through the tears. "I'm ready."

Ari burst through the door just as I'd gotten Waverly settled and Mason, the newest member of our group of family and friends, sleeping on her chest. I put up my hand.

"Congratulations. Go wash your hands before you touch either of them."

He blinked, Ari was in full on panicked new father mode. Mason wasn't biologically his son, but that didn't matter in our family groups. He loved him like he was. The doctor bled back into his gaze, leaving the terrified father nowhere to be seen. "Right. I'll sterilize."

"We're not going anywhere, love," Waverly spoke in a low voice. "And Diana has Emerson. He's safe down below."

"Right." Ari took off his coat, throwing it aside and rushing to the same sink I'd cleaned up in earlier. "You're okay. You are. You're okay." He spoke like he needed to say it a few times to believe it. "I wasn't here but Amber was and she is the best doctor, maybe ever. Certainly the fastest to ever become one. We couldn't believe it when you passed everything so fast."

I shook my head. "Good teachers." Even as I answered him, I kept my gaze fastened on the readouts from the med machine. Both mommy and baby were fine. They would stay that way and I'd watch to make sure for a while yet. "She was very brave, very strong."

Ari grinned at the sink. "Of course she was. She always is."

I wished I could leave and give them privacy. But someone had to read the screen, and Ari was really not to be trusted to be rational at the moment. I hit a button, sending the signal outside the room to the screen in the hall.

He walked over to his wife, kissing her soundly on the

lips before he stared down at their new arrival. "Why hello there. What did you name him?"

Didn't he know? She'd said it so fast when he was born I'd assumed they'd discussed it.

"This is Mason."

I closed the door, not surprised to find the all of the remaining Zansi Warriors, the Z as they were more regularly referred to, standing outside. They'd done this with the other babies born, too. The Z loved babies. Actually, the whole Chen Empire did. Any baby born here was automatically granted Chen Empire status, whether their parents were or not.

The fifteen Z stared at me, equal questions in all their gazes. It had freaked me out the first time they'd done this. Any kind of gathering of the Z used to mean violence to me. Now... it was complicated. They were loyal to my husbands and that meant more than anything else in the universe.

"Healthy baby boy."

Grins broke out on their usually stoic faces before they covered. Brenden spoke to me, quietly. The task always seemed to fall to him, as though he'd become their voice. "And his mother?"

"Mason is his name, and Waverly is well. You guys all know Ari by now. He's in there. Thanks for getting him, Brenden, and I'm going to give them some privacy by watching out here."

Someone cleared his throat and a second later, Wade Moyer stepped through the crowd. He was a doctor, and although I hadn't known him well on The Farm, since coming to Earth he had become my friend. He was recently back from time on a spaceship fighting in several battles. Once, Evander had imprisoned him while a man dubbed Doctor Disease impersonated him. He'd nearly killed

Waverly and ended up sending her through space and time in the process. Later, Sterling and Damian had rescued Wade on a mission to free a nearby planet being imprisoned by Evander.

The real Wade had come back. He was quiet but really good at medicine and devoted to taking care of his brother and sister who he was solely responsible for since the death of their parents.

"Need help, Dr. Chen?"

With Cash and Lewis gone, it was Wade who'd officially made me a doctor two months before. I'd been an intern until today, needing to be supervised by one of the other doctors. None of this was the way it was usually done, but unusual times called for unusual measures. Today, I'd earned my right to treat patients alone.

I pointed to the screen. "Just going to monitor."

"When was the last time you slept?" Wade looked at the monitor with me and lowered his voice. "And you're overdue for your own treatments."

I lifted my brow. "Slept? Does anyone sleep? It's constant. I think we need to get Waverly and the baby out of here sooner rather than later. I hate to move them just yet, but they need to go down below to the safety zone. And as for my treatment, I'll say what I've said before, there are more important uses of the med machines right now."

Wade turned to look at the Z Warriors. "Could you guys give me a minute to speak to Dr. Chen?"

None of them moved. It was Brenden who answered again. "If you have concerns for Dr. Chen's health, then we need to be aware of them. We can see to it that she gets what she needs. It is our solemn, sworn duty and our privilege to see to Dr. Chen while the Masters Chen are away."

I held up my hand. The secret of my infertility was not

a secret anymore. Hadn't been for some time. I had to explain my time in the med machines or the Z freaked out. My condition was painful but not life threatening, at least not yet.

"I'm fine. Wade is concerned with my pain. That is very kind of him but this isn't life or death."

The other doctor shook his head. "Maybe not yet. But if you leave it too long, it could eventually result in emergency surgery and a life or death situation at that point. You're lucky you were okay as long as you were without treatment. Things are clear now. No current emergencies. Waverly is doing fine. Ari can watch his wife and new baby if you point out he has to. And I can put you in the med machine, give you your treatment, and then, while the coast is still clear, you can recover from the treatment. Don't make me get Ari to sign off on benching you for days."

I sighed. "You'd do that, wouldn't you?"

"You have to take care of yourself so you can take care of others. I have to remind myself of this constantly. Trust me, I get it."

Wade had secrets. As far as I knew, he didn't have medical conditions he treated himself for. I wasn't going to ask him in front of the whole parade of Z. I had to have my personal life open for inspection, it came with being married to Amari, Hunter, and Shane. Wade didn't.

"Okay. Let's do this."

The med bay buzzed with machines. Only one third of them were in use so Wade was right. It was an easy night. Of course, we could have a hundred ships of wounded show up any minute. I shivered. I couldn't let myself think like that or I'd never get in it.

"Are you going to remind Ari to move Waverly?" I asked Wade as I chewed on my thumbnail.

"Already done." He grinned. "You'd think I hadn't done this for the last five years."

I shrugged. "Sorry. I'm pretty much alone here as the only doctor. The medical assistants are great and so are the three nurses, but since you officially made me one of you, it's been just me."

Wade nodded. "I know. I'm not leaving again. It's too much with just you, not since we officially became med bay central for this war. I'm thinking of asking Ari to reconsider being with the resistance and coming back here full time. Or bringing Lewis back from the outpost. What do you think?"

The truth was there just weren't enough doctors in the universe. "Everything they're doing matters where they are."

"I know. So it's you and me, Amber." He looked over his shoulder to where Brenden glared at him. The Z did not like when people used my first name. I had a life filled with dichotomy. As the wife of the Chens, everyone associated with the Chen Empire spoke to me in polite tones. As Paloma's baby sister, everyone from the Farm called me Amber. The former was bothered a lot more by the change than the latter.

I climbed into the machine. I hated this part. Still, I knew who I'd dream of. Amari, Hunter, and Shane. Oh, how I missed them. I'd once fled the galaxy to escape my life here. Now, I'd do anything just to have them with me.

I had to be brave. I wasn't ever going to be the version of Mrs. Chen my abusive mother-in-law had wanted, but I could be the best one I could manage on my own. Everyone on this side of the galaxy struggled right now, everyone bled, and everyone worried. We'd all made sacrifices, and the best I could do to honor them was keep up a brave face. I didn't do it because of some false idea of what a woman should be; I did it because it mattered to me to do so.

Wade closed the lid.

———

I woke up fast. The lid was open and an alarm blared. I tried to sit up. "How bad?"

The room tilted left and Wade put a hand on my shoulder. "It's only two ships and I've got it under control. Stay down, I'm sorry the alarm blared as you were waking. Don't get up too fast."

I nodded. "I'm okay?"

"Treatment went great. Brenden is here to take you to your room to rest. Go with him."

As if on cue, the Z Warrior appeared next to me. "I'm here, Dr. Chen. I'll get you home safely."

I knew he would.

We didn't talk on the way outside as we made our way to the entrance to the underground compound that was now the home of the Chen Empire. My husbands had forethought and they'd designed things to manage this war. No one lived in the mansion now, it was a constant target, and the anti-bomb measures were failing. Soon, the home I'd hated but now missed like I'd lost a phantom limb, would be gone.

I stared up at the sky. "It's beautiful tonight."

He nodded. "It is. Did you spend a lot of time outside in your other home? On The Farm?"

The Z almost never asked me about that place, as if pretending I hadn't vanished for two years would make it that way. The big scandal I'd pushed on everyone. "No, it wasn't safe there either. I want safe."

I was never that coherent when I first woke up. Poor Brenden had put up with this five times now.

"I want safe, too." He nodded. "Do you know if Chrissy liked to be outside?"

Chrissy? It took me a second. "The nurse?"

She was a very smart, talented nurse who helped us a ton. She'd come from a farming community on the edge of the Dark Planets and escaped a wife broker who'd wanted to sell her to someone.

"That's right."

I stopped walking. "You like her. I knew it."

Brenden's eyes widened. "Dr. Chen, we need to get you inside."

"You. Like. Chrissy." He wasn't getting out of this so easily. "And that's good because she likes you, too."

His mouth fell open. "She does?"

"Yes, of course she does. She asked me about you weeks ago. I told her it was complicated with the Z Warriors but I'd keep my ears open to see if you were thinking along those lines or still in self-deprivation mode."

Brenden winced. "You said *that*?"

"No, of course not." I grinned. "I told her I'd find a way to gently inquire if you were thinking about her. I haven't had you alone to do so before now. There were all those crisis nights."

He let out a breath. "Sometimes your sense of humor goes over my head. Yes, please tell her I like her. She wouldn't be opposed sometime in the future when it's safe to going on a date with me?"

"I'm sure she wouldn't." I patted his arm. "You could even take her outside."

A ship zoomed overhead followed by another. Brenden was right. We should probably get inside. I let him lead me the rest of the way, stopping at the bottom of the stairs to stare at the waterfall in front of me.

Leave it to Hunter to put everything that needed to be kept safe in the same place. I'd heard that this had actually been hidden like this since the bombs, but had Hunter made it even safer. The Chens cared about the water and in front of me was the waterfall that survived when most of Earth didn't. Clean, running water. Saving it, preserving it, had been the goal of the family forever and had made them rich beyond anyone's wildest dreams. In front of me was why there was a Chen Empire at all.

"It's beautiful," Brenden spoke in a soft tone. "Strikes me every time I come in and out."

"For me as well. I didn't get it when I first lived here. What was the big deal about this water? I never came to see it. All those years, never." I'd wasted a lot of time.

Brenden side-eyed me. "You were a little busy getting your ass kicked."

I laughed, covering my mouth. "Yes, that's true, and what you said shouldn't be funny. But it is."

He shook his head. "I never understand your sense of humor."

"I'm not sure, but I think that up until recently I didn't have one."

In my room, Applesauce waited for me to snuggle in my bed. I'd wanted to ask Brenden a question for some time, and since I was loopy, I did. "How did it work out the fifteen of you ended up here, not going?"

He smiled at me. "We're *your* guards, Amber." His use of my first name wasn't lost on me. He was trying this out because he'd heard Wade do it earlier would have been my guess, since they'd never listened to me when I told them to call me Amber in the past, to the point that I'd stopped requesting it.

"We go where you go. If you left, so would we. But if you're here, we're here. I'm in charge of your protection, as you know. I think Master Amari thought you would respond okay to me since I hadn't been here when you were hurt."

Why hadn't I understood this before? "All fifteen of you? That's a huge amount. My mother-in-law didn't have fifteen guards."

"It's wartime and you've already been hurt. The Z will not let that happen again. Fifteen seemed the right number."

I sighed, sitting on the bed. "Stuck with the weird, inappropriate Chen wife... I'm sorry."

"Amber." He made a face after he used my first name again. Informality didn't taste good. "Dr. Chen." He tilted his head in acknowledgement. "Every one of us volunteered. And we would again. Look around. This place would be gone without you. I think you might be keeping the entirety of the Chen Empire remaining here alive through the sheer force of your will alone. Add to that you are now a full-fledged doctor. We are proud to be your guards. I don't know what the Mrs. Chens were supposed to be before. She was a wicked old lady when I was young. You redefined the role. Keep doing what you're doing."

With his words still banging around in my ears, I crawled into bed, missing the men who had made me first Mrs. and now Doctor Chen like a giant hole in my heart I'd never fill.

A KNOCK SOUNDED and I woke up, groggy and disoriented. I hadn't slept long enough. If something was very wrong, I was going to have to medicate myself awake to replace the med machine drugs still warping my system.

The knock again.

"Yes. Come." I pulled the blanket to my chin.

Brenden rushed in. "Dr. Chen."

"What's wrong? How bad is it?" I got to my knees. "I need a minute to pull myself together. "

He shook his head fast "Nothing bad. I thought you should know right away. Sorry, it's just that Master Shane is here."

Here? That didn't make any sense. "Is he hurt?" I scrambled up. "I'm coming. Tell Wade I'm going to dose and be right there."

"Dose with what? No, I'm not hurt." Shane walked into the room. He patted Brenden on the shoulder. "I got this."

The Z Warrior nodded before he exited the room, closing the door behind him. My breath caught in my throat, and I thought I might have squealed for a second before I covered my mouth. I wasn't reacting to Shane being back in what probably would have been deemed a formal, correct manner. I wasn't sure what I was doing.

I drank in his dear face. He looked good, healthy but tired. There were dark circles under his eyes, but that was true for all of us these days. His hair had gotten a little longer, a little messy looking. It was adorable. His shoulders were still broad, the shine to his hair remained the same, he hadn't... lost any limbs.

He moved because I couldn't, taking me in his arms so gently I couldn't help my cry.

"Hello there, gorgeous." His strong arms were steady. Shane smelled right. I shook. "I think you missed me."

I lifted my head. "I'm so glad to see your face."

He wiped the tears trailing down my cheeks with his thumbs. "I'm so glad to see your face, too. What were you going to dose yourself with?"

"Oh, doesn't matter." I kissed him because I could. His lips were soft—they always were with Shane—and reveled in the feeling of the slight bite of his whiskers against my face. He kissed me back, picking me up so I could wrap my arms around his neck and my legs around his waist. I kissed and kissed and kissed him. I couldn't stop. Too many months without him, worrying he was dead whenever I let myself even think along those lines, and now the surprise of his sudden arrival undid me.

He laid me down on the bed as he finally pulled his mouth from mine. "Is this an okay time in the month for us to be doing this? I tried to keep track in my head of when your treatments should be. I thought about you every free second so that was one of the things I charted in my mind. But then we had a couple of weeks that blended into days because of the battles and I think I might have lost it. Just because I'm here doesn't mean you have to be in pain."

I kissed his nose. "I had a treatment about eight hours ago. I missed some, moved some. It's not always convenient for me to have them done. Other people need help more than me."

He scrunched up his face. "Then you should be sleeping. I wondered why Brenden took off like a bat out of hell to come down here. He must have wanted to give you a second to try to rouse. I thought you might be hurt and no one told me. I chased after him. None of it was well done."

I sat up, so close to him that our heads almost banged. "I don't want to sleep."

"Okay." He kissed me lightly on the lips and then smiled at me. "Amber, you can't know how it feels to see you right now. Some nights I wondered if I'd dreamed that you were still alive."

Our mouths fused together again. I pulled at his shirt, wanting to feel his skin beneath my fingers. He laughed as I got his shirt tangled over his head before I threw it aside. Applesauce ran into the corner to avoid being hit.

"Remind me I have to say hi to the cat when we're done. He deserves a hello of his own."

Shane was so sweet, all that kindness hidden beneath his serious exterior. I put my hand on his heart. It beat strongly beneath the pads of my fingers. I counted the beats. One. Two. Three. Four.

"Are you taking my pulse?" He nuzzled my neck. "Here's a hint. Right now it's racing. After I make love to my wife, it will regulate again and then probably slow when I take you in my arms to sleep for the night."

I pushed back to grin at him. "I'm a doctor now. Officially."

"Really?" The smile that lit his face would forever be in my memory. "That is such great news. I missed it. Fuck. Congratulations."

I wanted to hear all his stories, all the things happening to him, but I also wanted to make love to him, and he wanted me, too.

He pulled my nightgown over my head and dropped it at the foot of the bed. I tugged at his belt and then his pants, finally leaving him in just his briefs. He was hard, pressing into the fabric, evidence of how much he desired this. I cupped him on the outside of his briefs, squeezing him while I did.

Shane sucked in his breath. "Oh, fuck." He leaned his head back and closed his eyes. "Amber. This is really happening. It's not just in my mind. I never imagined it and had it feeling this good."

I hadn't even touched his skin yet. "Underwear, off. Please."

He lifted his lids. "Not yet. This will go too fast if I take them off."

Shane gently pushed me backward until I leaned against the headboard. Holding my eye contact the whole time he pressed my legs apart.

"Love? You don't have to. It's been so long," I didn't care if this was over fast. I wanted Shane. That was all that mattered.

"Amber, this is what I dreamed of. Well, all of it, but starting like this."

His mouth came down on my inner thigh, he trailed down my leg, all the way to my knee before he changed sides and did it again. I sighed. This was heaven. I wanted his lips all over me. I couldn't help it, I squeezed my own breasts.

Shane looked up as I squeezed my nipples. He moaned. "More of that. I am going to live off this for months."

He squeezed the opposite leg as his mouth came down on my thigh again. The buildup was extreme. Shane hadn't really touched me yet but that didn't last long. While he still kissed me, he pressed a finger into my vagina before finding my clit and squeezing.

Mimicking the movement on my nipple, I cried out. The duel pinch made my hips come off the bed. He squirmed closer, grinding his own hips into the bed while he did this. Shane kissed me on the insides of my thighs, not pressing in yet. Simple, gentle kisses heated my blood even more.

He licked me, moving his head not his tongue as he kept his tongue flat and unmoving the whole time. I cried out. It was the gentlest touch and it hit every nerve in my body, turning them on. He did this over and over before he stopped to bite down on my clit. I was so turned on, so ready for him, that I exploded in pleasure before I even knew it was going to happen.

I had no warning, the jolts wracking through my body. I dug my hands down the back of his head, but he didn't stop caressing my clit. Finally, I couldn't take anymore. I dragged his mouth to mine. As he kissed me, he pushed my hand away from my breast, replacing it with his own. That was perfect, I held onto his back, digging my fingers into his skin. I was going to leave marks on Shane, his skin could carry my presence long after he'd gone back to war.

He pressed inside of me, my insides squeezing around him. It felt like welcoming him home. Nothing should feel this good.

"Shane."

He pushed our foreheads together. "Stay with me. Right here. Like this moment never has to end."

I loved that idea. He moved inside of me slowly, his hips gently rolling our bodies together. I lifted my own to meet his thrusts. With each joining, we both cried out. This was pleasure. This was... everything.

He kissed me the whole time, our sounds joining like our bodies did. I didn't know how long we did this, but this was us loving each other. I could feel it in every ounce of my pores. Shane filled my every being.

"Amber." Shane pulled back. He had to be close. I didn't know how it was possible, but his whole body seemed to have hardened.

I kissed his chin, his cheek, his neck. Anywhere I could reach. "I've got you, love."

"Come with me." He kissed all over my face. "Need you with me."

I was close. As he found his own pleasure, it brought my own. I held onto him, knowing that I'd never have a moment like this again. Shane had come home to me. I was going to hold him every second I could.

―――

I listened to his heart, smiling at what he'd said earlier about how his heart rate would regulate and then slow. We were in the calming stage.

I raised up on my elbow. "Tell me all your stories. How bad is it?"

He turned his head to look at me. "I don't want my stories in here. There aren't any good ones right now. It's very bad, but it's almost over. Couple more big wins and Evander is running from Earth. It's going almost entirely the way Amari predicted." He yawned. "We all just have to live through it."

I laid my head back down. "Keep doing that."

"I'm coming back home and then I'm never leaving again." He kissed my temple. "So how long has it been since you've seen the other two?"

"What? Same as you, five months."

Shane shook his head. "Really? I would have thought for sure one of them would have swung through here. They've not been back? I thought it was just me."

"Hard to communicate out there? Not only here?"

"We can't get through here. Hunter is working on it. So I didn't know that the defenses are down and you all had to move underground. But we're careful what we share up there. I wouldn't want anyone to know I was coming here because it might put you at risk. They're not sharing that info either."

That made sense. "How long?"

His face fell. "Only until tomorrow. We're grabbing supplies and going back out."

"Thank you for coming here, Shane. I didn't know how much I needed to see you. I'm trying really hard to be strong like you guys."

He kissed the end of my nose. "Some days I'm not so strong. You're amazing. Just be you. All will once again be well. I know it."

I yawned. "Sorry."

"Sorry? You were supposed to be asleep this whole time. Go to sleep. I'm staying with you."

I snuggled against him. There were few things in life that I loved more than cuddling in bed. I let his heat wrap around me.

I woke up to my tablet going off. Shane slept, his eyes

closed, his head facing away from me. He'd not heard the dinging, which meant he must have been really out of it. When was the last time he'd slept? I grabbed the tablet. Wade hated to bother me, but there were five ships coming in all with injured.

He needed me.

I swung my legs over the bed and quietly made my way over to the chest of drawers. I grabbed my only clean pair of scrubs and put them on. Shane didn't move. He must have been exhausted. I wasn't much better myself.

I contemplated taking the adrenaline dose but it seemed like a bad idea. That really needed to be saved for emergencies since the side effects could be so bad. I'd take it with me if I needed a hit later. That sounded bad even in my own head.

I left Shane asleep, locking the door behind me, but I needn't have bothered worrying about his safety. There were ten Z standing in the hall with Matt, who was often there in the morning while Brenden slept.

I nodded at them. "Shane is out cold."

One of them, whose name I didn't know for sure but I thought might be Todd, answered. "That's not surprising. He never sleeps. I think it might have been a week since he did."

That bothered me both as his wife and as a doctor. "Leave him be unless you have to go, okay? Otherwise, if he sleeps all day, let him."

"Yes, Mrs. Chen." Todd nodded.

"It's Dr. Chen now." Matt smiled at me. "Everyone is very proud."

"Oh." Several of the Z looked at each other. My own guard might be used to things but that didn't mean that the entirety of the old boys' club around here was going to be thrilled. That was okay. They could all screw themselves if they didn't like it.

I took off toward the medical area, Matt hurrying to keep up with me. "Did you have a good night?"

He nodded. "You?"

"Top ten nights ever."

━━

Arriving amidst the horror of alarms, blood, and swearing made it clear it would be the day from hell and the sun wasn't even out yet.

Wade glanced up from where he operated. "Sorry, I called Ari, but he hasn't answered yet."

"They're probably deep in the depths of baby. I'm here. We'll get this done, you and me."

The nurse Chrissy entered the room at that moment, and I grinned. I was going to handle that, too. Everyone should have love like I did to come home to. If I could help spread it then I'd really feel like I'd done something for the universe.

I washed my hands. It was time to save lives.

━━

"Amber." Wade passed me a pill. I understood what he was saying. We had hours still ahead of us. With eight hours behind me, I was going to need the help.

I nodded. Wade hated this stuff. If he was giving it out then he must have been concerned. "We're both going to crash as soon as this is over."

"Yes."

Ari rushed into the room just as I swallowed down the

pill. He groaned. "That kind of night? Fuck. Sorry. I just saw the messages. I had it turned off. The baby is... not sleeping through the sounds of life. I had Emerson, and I'm sorry. The Z told me you had to leave Shane. I'm sorry."

"No one dies today." We all made sacrifices.

Ari grabbed one of the pills. "Let's get this done."

I'd taken care of two more patients before Shane called my name from the doorway. I whirled around. I was covered in blood. I couldn't even hug him because I'd have made a huge mess of him.

He leaned in the doorway. "Can you take a second?"

I looked around, Ari nodding at me, while he took over my spot. I ran to Shane, stopping right before I got to him. "I'm sorry."

"No, the guys told me there was a huge amount of injured. You were where you needed to be. I slept most of today and helped the guys get the stuff ready on the ship. I had to see you before I left again. Look at you in here. Running things. I'm just... blown away by you."

I waved my hand. "Stop. You're saving the universe."

"So are you." He leaned over and kissed my neck. "You smell so nice. Last night was amazing. I love you. I don't think I said that and it should have been the first thing out of my mouth. Then I should have said it over and over and over."

My hands shook with wanting to talk to him. "I'm dying to hug you."

He kissed me, keeping his body from touching me. "I love you."

"I love you more. Be safe. Come back."

He smiled at me, and I tried to memorize it so I'd never forget. "See you soon. Weeks now. I promise."

I was going to hold him to that.

"If you see Jackson, Canyon, or Rohan tell them they have a new son."

His smile was fast. "I'll do that. We need babies around here. Lots of after war babies."

A split second after the words left his mouth, his smile fell. There might be babies but they wouldn't be mine. "My love, I didn't..."

I interrupted him. "I know. Of course you didn't. I know you love me. And yes, there need to be lots of babies."

He kissed me again. "I wouldn't make you sad for anything. I'd sooner cut out my eyes."

"The only thing that makes me sad is you leaving. But I'm going to be happy you're coming back. Be safe, my love."

———

Days could become weeks in no time. I was dragging, but I didn't want to take another pill. The idea made my stomach turn. In fact, everything made my stomach turn. I had to get back in the med machine, and I didn't want to do that either, but I was going to because I didn't want another lecture. The Z were now following the schedule, with orders from Shane to do so. If I didn't get in, I was going to hear something about it.

It was a quiet night. The first since Shane had left. The war might almost be over but the casualties were huge on both sides.

I was just about to tell Wade to turn the thing on when Paloma stumbled into the room. "Amber."

The horror in her voice made me rush over. "What's wrong?"

"Something's wrong." She pointed down. "My water has broken, and it's too early."

It was. She wasn't wrong. Six weeks too early. My sister had problems with Ben's pregnancy, too. She'd had a blood clot requiring him to come a few weeks early. We'd seen no evidence of this, and I'd checked her yesterday.

"Come sit down."

Wade walked over, sticking on the machine. We both looked up. Paloma was in labor. Her water had broken and the baby was coming. Early.

The proximity alarm went off. There were ships coming in. Ari was below ground again, and it was just Wade and me.

He pointed at me. "Take your sister. Go stay with her. Save the baby."

"Save the baby?" Paloma's voice squeaked.

That had been a poorly timed phrase. I shot him a look, and he winced.

"Come on," I took her hand. "My love, you're going to have to walk a little bit longer. We're going to Artemis."

I didn't know who was up there. I had to take her someplace safe. The old ship was on the ground, not deemed worthy for this battle. That was fine. We'd be alone on it and we could have my nephew in private. There were two med machines. One old, one new. If I had to operate on Paloma, then both she and the baby could heal.

This was when I wished for Cash. For Lewis. For Dane. Oh, I'd take Dane any second now. A preemie. I didn't have one under my belt yet. Newborns on time were scary enough.

"Amber," Paloma's voice shook, reminding me I already had a patient and I had to stop calculating and focus on her.

I hugged her. "What did you do with Ben? He has to meet his little brother very shortly."

"He's with Diana. It's too soon."

I nodded. "We can fix it."

I would. I was going to make all of this okay.

———

I hoped that for the rest of my life I never had to do something as scary as deliver Paloma's preemie in the middle of a firefight with more injured showing up every minute.

I had to operate. There were rules about who we operated on, specifically family, and reasons for that. Wade should have done it, but by the time I realized it was operating time, he was too involved with the people coming off the ships. With no choice, I'd done it.

Now, as Aaron slept in one med machine that developed his lungs and helped him grow, Paloma sat in the other.

I sunk to the floor.

I'd really never felt so alone. What if I'd lost my sister? What if I'd lost Aaron who looked just like Ben to me, only startlingly small and new? What if... what if... what if?

"Dr. Chen." Brenden poked his head in. "Is there anything you need?"

Actually there was. Wade needed me as soon as I could get there but preemies had to be watched.

"Are there two Zs around who are not fighting and who could watch these machines? I have to leave Artemis." I actually had never felt better to leave them anywhere. There was something about Artemis. Some of my favorite people in the universe had been kept safe here, including me. Paloma had lived on Artemis for a while. The ship would take care of her. Hell, I was crazy. I was personifying the ship.

Brenden nodded. "I can. Matt can."

"Thank you." I was so tired, and I couldn't figure out if I was hungry or nauseated. I walked him to the machine and showed him what levels I wanted to see. "If anything changes, you call me immediately."

"We won't let anything happen to them. He's one of us now, and she's your sister. We consider them family."

I put my hand on his arm. "When this is over, I'm going to meditate for hours. I keep saying I'm going to and I keep not doing it."

The Z Warrior shook his head. "You didn't grow up with my father. You'd never have missed a morning. It's ingrained from birth. And I'm taking Chrissy out tomorrow. Unless we have more firefights." New babies. New loves. There really might be a future.

I ran to the med bay. It was chaos. That was okay. I'd make order out of it. I was good at that. My fellow doctor operated with a laser. "That you, Amber?"

He didn't look over. "It's me, Wade."

"Good. Listen, when this is over we need to talk about that woman you have in cryogenic sleep."

Sienna? "I check on her every other day."

"Right. I check on her every day."

He did? This was news for me. According to future Ari who visited me on Artemis, Sienna would eventually be Wade's patient. I didn't know how or when that happened. I washed my hands. "Something up with her? Brenden is going to call me if there are any issues with Paloma or Aaron."

"Good. I can help, too. I'm almost done, and I might need a break. When are you planning on waking her?"

That was a good question. I grabbed one of the patients from the waiting area. "Maybe never if this is the world.

Should I wake her up so she can suffer this hell with the rest of us?"

Wade made a sound I couldn't identify. Nausea roiled through me. Okay, when this was over, I was going to bed. Then I'd meditate. I would. Maybe.

I SAT on the floor drinking tea and watching Paloma's med machine readouts. There was nothing I wanted more in the world than to take a nap, but I wouldn't leave her until I was sure she was settled and I could leave her in the care of a nurse who would stay with her. Aaron was going to need more time and that was going to be hard on Paloma.

How could I help her with that?

My tablet beeped. I looked down. Someone was trying to reach me from outside of this compound. My heart rate kicked up. Did we have access? Was communication restored? I hit the button, and although at first it was fuzzy the image of Hunter's face stared back at me.

I cried out and then forced calm. He wasn't here like Shane had been, and I'd blown that reunion. I wouldn't spoil this.

"Well, there's my Amber's face." He touched the screen. "I've wanted to see that for six months."

A month. Had it really been that long since Shane was here? I guessed it had been. "Hunter. You fixed it."

"I had to rebuild the whole array. Big fucking mess.

Took twice as long as it should have because we kept getting fired on. Anyway, yes, it's done. You can look at my ugly face every day now when I call."

I didn't try to stop my happy tears. "Your beautiful face. I'm sure that's what you meant to say. I miss you."

He sighed. "Where are you? I don't recognize where you are."

"I'm sitting in the med bay in Artemis. I'm a doctor now."

His smile brightened. "That is great news. Why are you on Artemis?"

Hunter was a details guy. He was never going to let this go. "Well, Paloma almost died having Aaron yesterday. I had to operate on her. She bled and bled. I don't know why. No blood clot I could see. I almost lost her. There was a fire-fight happening at the same time. And," my voice wobbled so I paused until I could get it under control, "now I have my sister next to her preemie son, Aaron, in med machines. I'm sitting with them."

"They're going to be okay?"

I nodded. "Eventually. It'll be a few days. He's very small but strong."

He smiled at me. "I'm glad to hear that and I'm sorry you're all going through that. I can't think of anyone I'd rather have handle than you."

"You're just saying that. I've been a doctor for two seconds."

Hunter laughed; it was a great sound that I'd missed so much. "You love her. You were never going to let anything happen to her or to your nephew." He yawned. "Sorry. I think talking to you must be killing my adrenaline."

"Shane slept for most of the time he was here. I should

tell you to go sleep, but I want a few more minutes with you."

He widened his eyes. "Did my little brother manage to get home? Lucky bastard. Has Amari gotten home, too? Is it just me lost in the universe without you?"

I shook my head. "Just Shane and less than twenty-four hours."

"I'd take ten minutes." He sighed.

"Me too." I touched the screen. "You said you were under fire. Have you been mostly safe?"

"None of us are safe. Clearly, not you either. Can I assume you guys made it through the firefight? Defenses are holding."

I hadn't talked to him for six months so I hadn't had to face this. How much should I tell him about what was happening here? How much should I allow him to worry? "Hunter, you can't do anything about the situation. I'm thinking it might be best to not talk to you about it so you don't obsess."

He shook his head, some of his brown hair falling into his eyes. That was downright long for him. I wished I could brush it away. "I can't fix it now. But I might be able to help if I know there is a problem, or arrange for someone else to fix it."

"Is this secure?"

He sighed. "Probably not one hundred percent. Fuck, you're right. Don't tell me."

"You know what I was daydreaming about last week?"

My husband yawned again. I was going to have to let him go to sleep soon. "What? I love that you were daydreaming. What?"

"Do you think we could make a summer home we go to sometimes? Like away from here. Don't get me wrong. I love it here now. I know that makes no sense. I didn't love it when it was safe and pristine, and now I adore it. I'm weird. Anyway, a place where we could go, just the four of us and maybe two guards each." We'd never be entirely without the Z and as long as my guards stayed as they were that was fine with me.

He sat up. "I could build us a place. Do you have a quadrant in mind? I mean inside or outside of the Empire?"

"No. Just a daydream of looking at the ocean and seeing sunsets and drinking alcohol. Does that sound awful? The last part?"

He laughed. "Sounds good to me where I'm sitting. No alcohol there?"

"Non-essential."

"Well, fuck that." A thought dawned on me as I giggled at Hunter's response. "Can you get in touch with one of my brothers-in-law? The Sandlers? I mean, if this happened to me, if I was hurt, would you want to know or not know? I can't decide which is better."

Hunter ran a hand through his hair. "If you were hurt... I... I know what it feels like to not know that something is happening to the person you love. When we thought you were dead, any number of things could have happened to you and we'd have had no idea. When I think about that trek you made across the galaxy by yourself. Anyway, they need to know. I'll try to get in touch with them and see if there is anything else I can do."

My heart clenched and melted at the same time. I'd really thought they wouldn't care that I was dead or that it wouldn't bother them much. When I dwelled on that time, it made me heartsick for what I'd done. I hadn't thought I had a choice. I'd been wrong. Fortunately, we'd all moved past that, but it was always there. The two-year gap in our marriage. Hunter was going to see if he could reach the Sandlers.

"Thank you."

He touched the screen again. "I'm going to design and build us a summer home. I'm already calling it Amber's house in my head. I love you."

There it was. Those three beautiful words. "I love you, too."

"Then everything will be right in the universe. I should probably go. We only have so much power to do this, and I want to let the others here reach their people. I'm being selfish, but I don't want to end this talk. I've missed the very sound of your voice. Listen, I can't call every day. It's not safe and it's not always possible. But I'm going to try to write. Send you letters. Those can probably go through. If you want them."

I choked back my sob. There I was, ruining it again. I wiped at my eyes. "Sorry about the tears. I miss you. Everything is fine. Don't worry. If I want them? Yes, I want them. Every word. I'm so grateful for what you're doing and proud of you."

"Don't cry." He looked away. "I miss you, too. And we'll be together soon. Until then, we'll get to talk some now, and I'm going to send messages through to your tablet. Be safe." His gaze met mine again, and I was proud that I'd pulled it together. He touched his lips and then the screen again. "Love you."

I nodded. "Love you, too, and get some sleep. You need it."

"I will."

I got to my feet to check the med machines. Everything showed perfect. I stared down at the faces of my sister and her new son, who I already knew I was going to love as much as his brother. Ben was tucked in tight with Diana, watching movies with her daughter Helene. They were as safe as I could make any of them.

I'd never wanted to return to Earth, but now here I was somehow the caretaker of everyone here with me on this planet that had birthed humanity. Nausea hit me again. I had to be getting sick. I rubbed my arms. I didn't have any time for that so this was all just going to have to work itself out without illness overtaking me.

"Hunter's going to reach your husbands. Your newest love is getting stronger by the minute although he was already so strong at birth. Your Ben is with Diana who loves him like her own. I'm sorry I can't have the universe fixed when I wake you tomorrow but I tried to make the reasons your world turns as safe as I could make them. I love you, Paloma. All will be well."

I spent so much time assuring others of things I wasn't sure of myself.

―――

"Talk to me." I turned and then gasped as my brother-in-law Quinn Sandler strode into the room. He had a beard, which was a new look for him, but otherwise he was the Quinn I was used to. His gaze swept over the machines and then back to me. "Are they going to be okay?"

I hugged him. Quinn was the least huggy of the bunch of my brothers-in-law. But it was so nice to see him I had to do it just the same. He squeezed me for a second, and I found my voice before I stepped back.

"I'm just about to wake both of them. Paloma should be fine, now. She had a lot of blood loss by the time we got to Artemis. When she got to the med bay, she wasn't bleeding, but by the time we got here, she really was. I don't know why. I'm sorry. I couldn't... find out why but it stopped as soon as I delivered him. No obvious clots or tears in her uterus. Maybe Ari or someone else could have figured it out."

He waved his hand. "Don't do that. You would have found it if it was findable. Go on."

"He was obviously too early. Six weeks premature. Almost five pounds. His lungs weren't ready. That's the biggest problem right now. They developed overnight. She has recovered her blood loss. What we need now is for him to stay warm, gain weight, maintain his body temp. I don't know yet if he can do any of that. So it may be in and out of the machine. What I do know is he needs her and she needs him. And probably Ben. She needs Ben. And oh, Quinn, she needs you. They all need you and you're here. How are you here?"

He touched the med machine, staring down at Paloma and then at Aaron. "Your husband, he found me, which couldn't have been easy because I'm basically holed up in secret, tracking the heads of their fleet around and passing that information where it needs to go. But he found me, contacted me, and I got here just as fast as I could."

I looked at the time. "That was less than five hours ago." I couldn't believe even that much time had passed.

"Fast ship. It might be better to have one of my brothers. They're better in stress like this but I love her more than anything so I'm going to try not to fuck this up. And I want to see Ben. Can he come here?"

I thought about it. "Not yet. We really don't want Aaron getting sick and Ben is a perfectly healthy little boy loaded with germs, living underground, picking up everyone else's germs. You'll have to go to him."

"Got it." He nodded. "What now?"

I needed to wake them up.

―――

"Amber," Paloma's tired voice caught my attention. She sat on Quinn's lap, Aaron attached to her breast. It was such good news that he'd latched on with no trouble. Him gaining weight out of the machine was what we wanted.

The Z couldn't find Ari, and Wade was up to his ears in patients. He'd also let me know he wasn't wonderful with pediatrics. That wasn't helpful. Wade was funny. He alternated between the best person I knew and the grumpiest.

Maybe we were all that way.

"Paloma?"

I was leaving her with a nurse for the next hour. I had to go get a pill or lie down. Wade and I were going to have to bite the bullet and make a schedule. Neither one of us was going to be able to keep this up unless we got some sort of help. The Z were after me for my treatment but I think even they recognized I couldn't get in the machine while things were a non-stop chaotic fight to save lives.

"Thank you."

I shook my head. "Nothing to thank me for. I love you. And I think Ben can come when Aaron is in the machine, okay?"

"More than okay. Thanks for getting Quinn here."

That hadn't been me. "That was Hunter."

"Semantics. You told him. I'm too tired. Just thank you."

I nodded at the nurse. "Let me know if anything changes and put Aaron back in the machine in an hour. Okay?"

I was pretty sure the woman nodded back to me. I was

going to go take a shower and then find Ben and bring him so he could see his brother. Matt met me outside the med bay on Artemis, which meant that Brenden must be sleeping. What time was it?

I hurried to get to my room, stopping to make sure the water ran when I entered the underground living quarters. It did. The waterfall was still there. I didn't know why. Maybe it was because it was so darn old, but as long as that waterfall stayed functional, then somehow we would all be okay.

I put my hand out to touch the stream, something I'd never done before. It was cool to the touch.

"Your husband Master Shane does that every time he passes it. But I'm told he doesn't need to because he can basically smell if it's off." Matt spoke in a low voice. He rarely addressed me first. I must have been standing there long enough to make him nervous.

I nodded. "I've seen him do that. He has a real gift for the water. This will still be as it always was when they all get back."

That felt like a vow as I said it. I wasn't usually so... dramatic.

"It will." If Matt thought what I'd said odd, he didn't indicate it, which I appreciated. I made my way to my room. Applesauce met me by the door, letting me know in no uncertain terms what he thought of my long absence. He had an automated feeder and a machine that also cleaned his litter. It was my company he missed, and I felt the same for him.

I didn't have a lot of time but I spent ten minutes of it petting the cat. That must have been enough. He walked to the air vent, sat on it, and proceeded to clean himself. I followed his lead and took the shower I'd sought out in coming here.

I let the water rinse away my day.

—————

Ben stared at his little brother, a very serious expression on his face.

Quinn held him tightly, his nose pressed to his nephew's hair. They might not have been father-son but there was no sense of that in Paloma's household. They all loved that boy like he was their biological son, not one bit less than Clay, his actual father, did.

"What do you think?" Quinn asked him, sparing a look at Paloma.

She was asleep in the chair. I checked her readings, and they were strong. My poor sister just needed to sleep.

"He's my responsibility." Ben finally answered him.

I stared at Quinn. That was a new word for him as far as I knew. Quinn looked back at me. I shook my head. He hadn't gotten that from me. Maybe Paloma said that? But I doubted it. I didn't think she was sticking her three-year-old with that kind of job just yet.

Quinn squeezed him. "What makes you say that?"

"He just is. I've seen brothers, and I know how it goes now. I'm going to take care of him."

This was so cute. "Well, maybe you could help all the grown-ups take care of him a little bit. And then when you're older, he can be your playmate, and you can help him out when he needs it."

"I'm going to take care of him."

He was so darn cute. I...

An alarm sounded that jolted Paloma awake. Her blood pressure skyrocketed, and the machine yelled out an alert. Yes, we were all probably up there right at that second.

I jumped up. "Stay here."

Matt rushed in the room. He held his ear, obviously getting an update through the Z network. "Evander is on the ground, heading here."

"Fuck." I hardly ever cursed, but sometimes those words were called for and appropriate. "Matt can you fly this ship? It's old."

He blinked. "Yes, ma'am. I can."

"Good. Get them out of here. Somewhere nearby, but in the air. Safe. I know I'm asking the impossible, but this is my family, and I'm trusting you with them. Do you understand?"

He looked like he was going to argue, and then he stopped. "Yes, Dr. Chen. I'll do just that."

"Thank you."

I ran past him, not stopping for Paloma's yell. There were things to do and one of them was to get them out of here.

The Chens had kept the water running and safe for hundreds of years. I was the only Chen here. I was going to see to it that happened.

This was my job.

I got off the ship as the engines roared to life and nearly collided with Brenden in the process.

"Dr. Chen?" he shouted. "What are you doing? Where is Matt?"

I pulled Brenden with me. He was exactly what I needed. "We're under attack. He's saving my family. As I told him to do. Come on. We have to get to the water."

I thought he might have objected, but he didn't. "Can you reach Wade?"

"Yes." He touched his ear. "I can get to most people using this as long as they're in the area."

"Tell Wade he has to evacuate the med center. I can't help him. That water and the people there are my job. It's what the Chens do."

He nodded. "You honor us."

Normally, I would object to that phrase. I hated it. Honoring this, honoring that. But I had no time for that sort of thing right now. It wasn't an honor, it was my right as Amari, Hunter, and Shane's wife to take care of things here. I would hold this place for them so it was here when they got back.

"Will our forces hold?"

He winced. "I don't know. The ground forces here are weak. We've been uninteresting to Evander until now. Just people, not resources they need. Maybe they're turning here for the purpose of collateral damage."

I doubted that. "No. They want something. Evander is about business. Sandler Corporation wanted domination. That isn't Evander's way. Earth is a resource. People can be a resource if they're put to work until they're too old or too sick to matter. Otherwise they kill them to get them away from the resources." What did we have here? "They don't need water. There's plenty on Earth unless they eradicate it, and they aren't going to do that. They are resource seeking. They aren't moving here. They're taking things, taking over, and bringing them across the black hole. They've used up their resources over there. It makes sense to take ours while theirs recuperates and then they're going to do it again."

I'd stopped running. In the distance, I could hear the foray coming. Bombs. Guns. I knew these sounds too well lately. I had to think faster.

"What do we have?"

He pointed. "You. They want the Chens to stop. They take or kill you."

"No, I'm nothing to Evander. If I die, if I live, I'm just another person on an expense report. They don't care about people. They care about..."

Fuck. How could I have forgotten? All this time and I'd not focused on Sienna. They'd told me when I took her from that space station that Evander wanted her. She was a commodity to them. Why? I still didn't know.

"We have to move Sienna."

Brenden blinked, staring at me. "Who?"

She was a well-kept secret, so unknown that Brenden didn't even know. When I went to check on her, he thought I was looking at medical supplies.

"You're going to be very upset with me. Yell at me later."

He stared at me like I had two heads. "I would never presume..."

"Yes, you would." I tugged on his arm. "We have to go to storage. We have to move her."

"Dr. Chen, I don't understand..."

I had no time for this. "You will. Brenden you have to trust me. If we move Sienna, we can save the water, save the people. If they're tracing her, then we have to move her away. And fuck. Send a message to one of the guys. Tell them to call for help. Tell them to say that Evander is here. The signals are open. Someone will come."

I hoped.

The storage unit in the very back of the living quarters underground held mostly medical supplies, bedding, shelving units filled with air filters, rat traps, and Sienna

MacKinnon, who I had been charged with taking care of for nine months now.

"Is that a woman in cryogenic sleep?"

I nodded. "Yes it is. My husbands know. I had to keep her secret."

"Evander wants her." Brenden stated the obvious, catching up. "Where should we take her?"

"Onto a shuttle. I'll take her. I'll keep moving until we can figure something else out. They can chase me."

He shook his head but even as he did we grabbed the chamber together. It had wheels. That didn't make it any less awkward to move. We rolled her together down the hall. "There's no way in hell, Amber, that I'm letting you do that. I'll do that."

"You can't. She's sick. She might need medical help if something happens," I sighed. "It has to be me."

We nearly hit a wall. "Do you have any idea how dead I will be if I let you go up in a shuttle by yourself with this lady and you were to get hurt? Forget it, I wouldn't be dead. I wouldn't want to live anymore. You are my responsibility. The Z Warriors do not let the Chen wives get hurt. We have failed you over and over. You are brave to the point of distraction. You don't sleep or eat. You do for others constantly. I know I just called you Amber. Sometimes I slip because you seem so human and not like a... like a distant, cold, old woman who made my mother miserable."

He couldn't have been talking about me, he had to mean my mother-in-law. "Okay."

"So no, you may not..."

I collided with a solid figure behind me, shrieking. I whirled around. I didn't have a weapon, but I was sure that Brenden did.

With my heart in my stomach, I recognized Blaze, the

Super Soldier who had once convinced me to stop being a coward.

"Evander's coming. They want the girl."

I put my hands on my knees. "We've figured that out."

This was proving to be a very long day.

BLAZE RIPPED the chamber from me. "I'm taking her away from here. We have some troops on the ground. It might take a little, but we'll push Evander back. Sorry they got here at all. We didn't foresee this coming. Fortunately, we got the call from Quinn on Artemis and we came fast."

"You can't just take her." Wade rounded the corner. Was the entire world going to descend on the storage area? "She's not well. That's why she's still asleep. We don't even know what's wrong with her yet because we can't devote anytime to finding out since we're constantly under siege."

A muscle ticked in Blaze's jaw. "Then come with us."

Wade looked at me and then at Sienna again. "I can't take off with you. We're overwhelmed as it is."

"Don't you have the kids to look after?" His brother and sister counted on him.

He shook his head. "They're on Venus Colony in a school. I sent them off two weeks ago."

He had? Did I know that? "Okay. Wade, go. It's fine. Don't argue. Sienna needs help and she's your patient now."

As I said it, I realized that by doing so, part of what Ari

had told me would happen. Future Ari in my only experience with time travel told me that Sienna would be my patient and then at some point would become Wade's. There, it happened. In some ways, it was a relief.

"Okay. I'll come with you."

Blaze pulled the chamber along, Wade chasing after him. I ran behind. This was all lunacy.

"Got her?" A man I'd never seen before called out, running off a shuttle.

"Yes, and this doctor is coming with us." Blaze plowed ahead onto the shuttle.

The man stared at Wade. "Oh good. Another non Super Soldier. It'll be a relief. I'm Trenton. Hey, anyone seen my buddy Ari?"

Well, I still didn't know who he was, but apparently he knew Ari. That was good, I guessed. Trenton. Blaze wouldn't hurt Sienna would he? I ran toward Wade. "Take care of her."

He nodded. "I will. I'm sure we'll be back."

"Not necessarily," Blaze supplied.

I wanted to go back to having almost next to nothing to do with Blaze and his Super Soldiers. Canyon, Rohan and Sterling were nice. I didn't know about this man. I pointed at him. "I know you don't think highly of me, but mark my words, if anything happens to this woman, you will know pain. I promise you that."

He stared at me and then past me. I looked quickly. Brenden and three other Z Warriors stared back at him. Blaze nodded. "I think you would find a way to hurt me if I hurt you. I misread you, Amber. All those months ago. I would never call you a coward now."

"You called her a coward?" Brenden's voice didn't rise. If anything, it lowered.

I pointed at the shuttle. "See if you can find my sister while you are up there and see if they're okay."

"Today I am apparently taking orders from everyone. Yes, I'll do that. Good luck, Amber. I imagine we'll see each other again. I've become a big fan of your husbands. They're brutal."

I didn't know how I felt about that statement. Brenden pulled me backward. "How are you going to do any of this without another doctor here?"

"I..."

A mechanical scream filled the air, our only warning as a bomb detonated somewhere just above, throwing all of us backward. Too close. Too damn close. I hit the ground. My ears rang, and I tasted dirt and blood in my mouth. This was strangely reminiscent to Oceania blowing up. I coughed. That time I'd landed on my back, this time it was my shoulder.

Hands pulled me up as Brenden pointed behind him. The mansion had blown up. No, it had been bombed. I grabbed my head. We had to get inside, we had to protect the water.

I let the Z Warriors help me inside, trying to assess if any of them weren't okay. I couldn't really focus. I grabbed Brenden's arm. "Call Lewis and Ari."

The world went black.

———

I woke up with a light shining in my eyes. Ari stared down at me. "Well, you're seeing me. That's good news."

I groaned as my head pounded in time with my heartbeat. "Why haven't you given me something for the pain? All the med machines dead?"

"I can't." He set aside his light. "Well, I can give you something but not something that is going to take the edge off. It might just be better if I didn't."

That didn't make any sense. Or maybe it was just that given that I'd lost consciousness. My head pounded like I had a one-woman band performing. I was probably concussed and couldn't think straight. "Are other people more injured? Is that why I can't have the machine?"

"You can't have the machine because the medicine it will give you will not be good for the pregnancy."

I gripped my head. "What pregnancy?"

"The one you're having right now." Ari stared at me as I tried to make sense of what he said. "You're pregnant, Amber."

"She's what?" Brenden suddenly came into view. He was beat up, a huge cut down the side of his face.

Okay. So we weren't alone. Ari turned and glared at him. "I think I told you to stay in the hall."

"I don't stay in the hall when it comes to her health. This is wonderful news." His smile was huge. "The Chen Empire will celebrate even in this war."

I shook my head, which hurt. "This isn't good news."

"Yes, it is. I know things are rough right now, but we have reason to be hopeful."

He was being sweet. "The condition that I get in the med machine for once a month makes it highly probable I will miscarry this baby. I've lost one already. That was my mother-in-law's fault, but I would have likely lost it anyway. It's hard for me to get pregnant, but I can. Staying that way is going to be next to impossible. There are eight —yes just eight—recorded cases of successful pregnancies of live babies born to women in my condition. None of them took place during a war. I'd need constant monitoring. I can't have that. My husbands know. This isn't a secret."

If my head hadn't been pounding, I'd have stormed off and slammed a door right then. That wasn't mature or helpful, but it was what I wanted to do. Why hadn't I thought about this? It had seemed next to impossible. In all the years married and here, I'd gotten pregnant once. It hadn't seemed particularly likely it would happen now.

But then of course it was.

"Let me think on this." Ari put his hand on my shoulder. "I agree. A daily six hours in the med machine would be ideal but obviously not happening in this time of war."

Brenden cleared his throat. "This is Dr. Chen. She's the Chen wife. She can have a dedicated med machine and a team of guards."

"There isn't a staff to watch her. I didn't know it had gotten this bad here. Why didn't you tell me?"

I hurt too much to answer that question. He must have read how pissed it made me in my gaze because he held up both of his hands as if in surrender. "I contacted Lewis. He's coming back. I'll stay here. They're doing pretty well underground. I can back off."

Ari had been spending his time with the non Z Warrior resistance happening on Earth. We needed everyone. I pulled my knees to my forehead. It didn't help my headache. I felt so many things right now I couldn't handle any of them. Absolute terror ranked at the top of that list. I was pregnant, and I absolutely did not want to lose this baby.

"Let me think about this, Amber. Lewis is coming. What we need is Dane. He brought Diana back from being a Zombie. Sorry, that's a bad word but that's what it was. Then Cash and Lewis fixed it up even more that you can't even tell that she had the condition to begin with. You need one of them. They're better at this."

"My love." Waverly's voice filled the room. "You took nanos out of Canyon's eyes and rebuilt his eyes. I think you could do this, too. Sorry to eavesdrop, but no one is being quiet." She walked in slowly. "We'll figure this out, Amber. You're going to have a baby. That's wonderful news. Let's just hold onto that. Get in contact with your husbands. Not assume the rest. Surround the baby and you with as much positive energy as we possibly can."

Brenden pointed at Waverly. "What she said."

I wanted Amari—who I still hadn't heard from—Shane, and Hunter more than anything in the universe. Just a minute alone with them. But then I was being selfish. They were needed. There only was communication again because of Hunter. Countless people were going to have a future because of my husbands and the people with them.

"Let's look at the baby."

I sucked in a breath. "Right now?"

"Yes."

I knew what Ari was doing tapping on the medical tablet. I'd done it myself a few times. It was hard for me to look up at the screen on the ceiling. In fact, any movement was agony. Tears flooded my eyes. I hated crying.

Waverly tucked me against her side. "Amber, it's going to be okay. It should be Paloma here. I'm sorry."

"No." I waved my hand. "She's up in the sky. I sent her up there to be protected during the battle. Are they okay?"

Ari nodded. "They are. I heard from Wade. They met up with your sister. Everyone should be on their way back here. That was smart thinking."

Sometimes I had my moments.

"Now look at that, that's a wrinkle." Ari pointed at the screen.

I forced my gaze up. "What? Is it already ending?"

"No. There's two heartbeats." He pointed. "Two babies."

Okay, now I couldn't breathe. Two? There was no way they were going to make it. Waverly pressed her head down on my shoulder. "This is going to be okay."

I didn't know how much more hope I could hold onto. It might have been my pounding head and my concussion, but I'd lost all of it that I had to give.

Losing them... those two people who were temporarily inside of me... was going to break me.

———

Being concussed without the machine really, really sucked. That was my professional opinion. Stuck in the med bay, I stared at the ceiling. I couldn't read, couldn't particularly do anything but sit and watch Ari receive patients.

Eventually, he walked over holding my tablet. He handed it to me. "Try to get in touch with your husbands. You'll feel better. I promise you that." He pointed at me. "Don't roll your eyes at me. I know of what I say. I was once very, very low. And then Cash got blown up and almost died. I swore I'd pull my shit together and I did. I wasn't sure I'd ever be okay. I really wasn't. And then Waverly came and I was. We need the people we love. I've been missing my family like crazy. It makes the darkness come back. And then we need to remember the light. That's my advice to you. You've been doing a great job of pretending your darkness is no big deal, that all the things that happened are unimportant because of this shared disaster we're all existing in together. That is remarkable and correct in a lot of ways." He sighed. "But it's there, and now you have to manage what happened. I know you want these babies. We'll fight for them as best we can."

He pointed at the tablet. "Call. We can get through sometimes now. See if you can."

I stared down at the tablet. "I didn't think I should do screen time with my headache."

He winked. "Probably not. Few minutes won't kill you. Doctor's orders." He smiled and walked away.

I supposed he was right. My tablet was full of messages. Hunter had said he would write and it looked like he really had. I smiled. I'd read them later. I quickly typed out a message to him.

Hunter,

I haven't had a chance to read your letters. We were under attack. Maybe you heard? I'm not sure how much the news gets through or if it did. I got hurt, but I will be okay, eventually. I can't go in the machine to treat the pain because I received the news when I woke up that I'm pregnant with twins. You're the first person I'm telling, although it seems half the Empire was in the room with me when I got the news. So I'm sure everyone knows.

I'm afraid. Much more afraid of this than I've ever been of anything.

I'm afraid I can't keep them safe.

I wasn't going to bother you with this. You have enough going on. But Ari said it was important I tell all of you. Please don't worry. I'll keep it together. All will be fine at home. I will read your letters when I'm given permission to read again. The trouble with not being able to treat a concussion. I shouldn't even be doing this but... I am.

With my love,

Amber

I almost didn't hit send. Was it okay to burden him with this? In the end, I hit the button and tried not to overthink it. I needed to talk to Shane. Although they would belong to all of them, he was their daddy. I scanned down. My tablet to his tablet. Maybe he would get the message, maybe he would answer. I chewed on my lip.

Shane's face appeared. He rubbed at his eyes, and then he grinned. I must have woken him. "Hey, beautiful. We must have just moved into range. I was going to try later today. Hey, you look funny." His smile fell and serious, silent, unmoving Shane appeared in his place. "What's wrong? You're hurt."

"We were attacked. We came through okay. Called for help. The Super Soldier, Blaze, and some of his people arrived. It's a very long story."

He pointed at the screen. "Where were the Z with you? How did they let you get hurt?"

I rubbed the back of my neck. "They were with me. The bomb came down. We all got hit in the shockwave. There isn't much they could have done in that moment. Don't blame them."

A muscle ticked in his jaw. That was a huge movement for Shane when he went silent. "Now that you have treated others you need to put yourself in the machine and get better."

"I can't. That's why I'm calling. We're going to have babies. Two of them. Twins. Just found out. So I guess your visit was... ah... fruitful." Oh by the universe, that was such a stupid thing to say. I spoke faster. "And they can't treat the concussion. I wasn't sure if I should tell you but Ari said it was very important."

Shane's eyes widened. The silence was gone. "Babies? Plural? We're having twins?"

"Yes. Well, I'm pregnant. I mean, we know that I'm probably not having these babies." My voice broke, and I had to look away.

"Amber," Shane said my name with such forcefulness I had to look back. "I love you. And whatever happens, I love you. Is there anything you need that you don't have? That I can have sent to you?"

You. Hunter. Your brother Amari who seems like he vanished into the universe. "No. I have everything I need. Only time will tell now."

"I'll be home before the babies come. I promise. I'll hold you, and you'll be okay, right there with us."

I hoped he was right. The last time he'd been here he'd told me he would be home in weeks. That hadn't happened. I wasn't sure what was going on with the battles. I wasn't involved in any of that.

"I love you. Be safe."

He smiled. "Be good to yourself. Stay hopeful. Believe for me. I'm sending you lots of energy through the universe. If you can, meditate every day. I promise. It helps."

Meditate? Yes, I needed to make myself do that. It would help. I wouldn't love it, I doubted I ever would, but it would center me. Ari had been right about this. It helped to call.

"I love you." That seemed better than goodbye.

I tried to do what I had with Shane and reach out to Amari, but the signal was lost three times. He was leading the battles, he and Melissa Alexander. Maybe it was really good that he was unreachable. If he couldn't be found then maybe Evander couldn't find him either.

I sat back.

I did feel better. Filled up in a way that had emptied.

"Aunty." Ben Sandler ran into the room. I spun too quickly to look at him and dizziness assaulted me. Still, I smiled and scooped him up.

"You're back?"

"We're back." Quinn pushed the med machine holding Aaron into the room with Paloma walking slowly behind him. "Looks like you got beat up pretty badly here. Thanks for getting us to safety, Amber."

That was downright chatty for Quinn. I brought Ben to my face, kissing him. "I'm just glad Artemis can still fly."

"Yes, but not with us on it." Paloma plopped down next to me. "Blaze decided it would be smart to switch ships as a secondary precaution. We took the shuttle, and he changed onto Artemis. This was after he vented the cryogenic chamber into space so it couldn't be tracked."

I tried to jump up and Paloma grabbed my arm. "Whoa. What are you doing? Sorry. The girl wasn't in it. Wade took her out. She's in a med machine."

He took her out of the chamber? I grabbed my head, and Ari strode over. "Well, that shot your blood pressure right up. Paloma, your sister is concussed. She needs to take it easy, both for herself and the babies. Don't make her upset."

Paloma's mouth fell open. "Babies?"

"Shit." Ari shook his head. "I can't keep track of who knows and who doesn't."

I kissed Ben's cheeks. That would help. I wanted this. I did. I loved my nephews, but I wanted the two in my stomach. It was terrifying to even think that because it showed how much I had to lose. We were at war, everything could be lost. Shane's face when I'd told him...

Paloma squeezed me tightly. "This is great news."

I hoped she was right. I wanted it to be.

Ten days was a long time to not be allowed to do anything but sit around the med bay and take treatments, especially when I was obviously needed. Lewis had returned, which was a great help, but we had the fallout from a huge battle in quadrant seven. There were injured everywhere.

Ari had finally released me. The sun was shining and the cold air that had come to the region wasn't too sharp yet. I rubbed my arms but strolled around the compound, Brenden with me.

"How did the date go?" I shouldn't have asked him. I should have minded my own business, but I did it anyway.

He smiled. "Really, really well. How many did we lose?"

This was the first time he'd asked me for a death number. "From the Chen Empire or the war in total or the last battle?"

"Let's start with the Chen Empire."

"I think the last count I heard was several hundred people." It might be more than that. Realistic counts weren't going to come until this was over.

Brenden nodded. "You had your treatment today. Right?"

I had. I was in and out of the med machine, conscious the whole time, while it removed my scar tissue and hopefully left the fetal tissue alone. Several hours a day that would only become longer as this went on.

I'd taken to counting down in my head from three thousand. It was easier than thinking about the people I wasn't helping who cried out in pain while I used a med machine the other doctors could have used to treat them.

Was I really allowed to be this selfish?

"I want to go look at what is left of the mansion."

Brenden winced. "Not much. I think it'll have to be broken down to its pieces and we'll go from there."

"Let's look."

We turned in that direction. "It's just a pile of rubble."

He was right. There wasn't anything left to it, and I'd never been more grateful that we'd moved everyone out of it so quickly. There wasn't anyone in it they could have hurt. I touched the brick in my hand. "They built this monstrosity right after the bombs went off. And a bomb took it down."

"Not the same kind of bombs. At least Evander hasn't pulled them out yet. But then again, the nuclear bombs would take down the resources. Not so much profit."

That was when I spotted her. At first I thought I must have been hallucinating. My mother-in-law didn't live here anymore. She'd been banished to Sandler Space for what she'd done to me. And yet there she was.

Callie Chen had always been a beautiful woman. Dark haired, dark eyed. Her sons resembled her, although the bones structure of their faces were different, much more the portrait of their father I had seen.

My whole body went cold.

"Brenden, do you see her?"

He turned. "Who?"

The second he recognized Mrs. Chen, the Z warrior stiffened. "Amber, get behind me."

"Now, now. I hoped you would come here. I've waited for days. I told myself that at some point the illustrious Mrs.

Chen... oh, I'm sorry, it's Dr. Chen isn't it? Well, whatever, would have to come outside. You do like to hide away like the creature of the dark you are, Amber."

I stepped behind Brenden. Someone else might argue. I didn't want that woman coming anywhere near me. I touched my stomach.

"Mrs. Chen." I knew he wasn't speaking to me. "You're not welcome here. You need to reboard your vessel and leave."

She laughed. That wicked sound that made my stomach clench. Oh, how I hated this woman.

"I'm not going anywhere, young man. I'm not alone."

Like they came from the shadows, four men who had to be Z Warriors seemed to appear next to her. Brenden touched his ear bud. "We have a problem. The former Mrs. Chen and four disgraced Z are here. They're at the old mansion. Come fast."

I didn't have to be psychic to know what would happen. The four Z jumped in the air at Brenden. He rose in the air. The way they could all move, it never ceased to stun me. I watched for a second before I turned to run. I would get Brenden help.

The longer the Z practiced, the stronger they got. There was simply no way my guard could take four of hers. They were like blurs of light. I wouldn't have Brenden's extinguished.

A jolt of electricity took me down. I didn't even know what she'd hit me with.

I WOKE UP FAST. Unlike other times when I might have been confused, I knew exactly where I was and who I was with. The sound of the space shuttle confirmed my worst fears. My lunatic nightmare of a mother-in-law had me with her, and I was no longer on the ground in the Chen Empire.

I sat up, grateful to see she hadn't strapped me down.

Brenden must have been dead. I couldn't even fathom that, but my horror at the idea of his too early demise had to wait until I dealt with my current situation. Why wouldn't she have restrained me? The answer came fast. She had no reason to think I'd ever fight her back.

"Their deaths were in serving you, all they ever wanted." A male voice spoke to my left, and I let myself stretch to see who was there.

By the controls to this small shuttle were two men I hadn't seen before they'd attacked Brenden. The other two weren't anywhere to be found, and if I understood what they said correctly, then it seemed the other two were dead. Had Brenden managed to take them out before they killed him or had I missed a battle while I'd been knocked out?

My mother-in-law sat in a low-cut dress that showed off more of her figure than I ever wanted to see, her head tilted to the side. "I never wanted any of you to die for me. It's her who should die."

Well now, she was most certainly speaking of me. I jumped up. All three of them startled, my mother-in-law coming to her feet.

"I see she decided to finally wake up."

She used to do this all the time. Knock me out and then be surprised when I didn't rouse immediately. Why hadn't she put me in the med machine? I looked around. There wasn't one. That was illegal. All vessels set up for space travel were required to have a med machine on board. If this one didn't have one, then it wasn't legal.

That made sense. No way had they managed to procure a shuttle to take them to Earth, from which she was banned, and have it be legal. I bet this was the best they could do.

"Callie Chen. I should have known I wasn't done having to deal with you."

She stormed toward me. "Having to deal with me? How dare you speak to me that way. You were never fit to be a Chen wife."

I'd heard this over and over again. Next, she would have had the example of what I did wrong and the beating would start. This time she thought she was going to kill me? Well, fuck this bitch and the shuttle she came in on. If I was going down, then she was going with me.

I launched myself at her. "You're right, Callie, I was not a good Chen wife back then. But don't you worry, I've improved myself greatly."

I'd never actually hit anyone before. Of all the things I'd learned over the years, how to deliver a punch wasn't one of them. Some things apparently could come naturally. I hit her, hard.

Strong arms yanked me off her, but not before I kicked her one more time in the face. "What's the matter, Callie? Can't take your lessons? How stupid are you?"

The Z Warrior who had picked me off her slapped me hard across the face. Now, this I was used to. My cheek stung. I lifted my head. I'd never beat back this man. But that didn't mean I couldn't get a few kicks and bites in before I was done.

The ship jarred left and we all flew that way. I struck the table I'd been laid out on before an explosion blared through my ears. Callie took that chance to rush at me, her hands going for my throat. I was on the floor. How had she managed to get herself up so fast?

I didn't think, I just reacted. I kicked her again in the face. Once. Twice. Blood gushed everywhere now. She managed to wrench free, and even though the ship bayed left, then right again, and things were exploding everywhere, we rolled around like we were on flat ground. She got some good hits in on me, but I was younger, fitter, and I had years of pent up hate for this woman to drive me forward.

I banged her head on the ground into the table. I banged her over and over until she stopped moving, until liquid brain matter came out of her ears, until I realized I'd killed her.

I let out a squeak as reality rushed back through my haze of anger. I had just killed my husbands' mother.

I didn't have time to dwell on what I'd done. The taller of the two men ripped me backward, screaming in my ear. I looked up at him in time to see death in his gaze. I'd killed my mother-in-law, but my days of breathing were over. I closed my eyes.

I fell backward, my lids opening, and I somehow managed to catch myself. The other former Z Warrior lay dead on the floor, his eyes unseeing.

My eldest husband had the other, the one who'd grabbed me by the neck. "No one touches my wife and lives to see another minute. Besides, we all thought you were dead anyway, Vondrey."

"She killed your mother." He could barely speak for Amari's hand around his throat.

"Good."

Amari dropped the man onto the ground. I leaned against the table staring, as Amari turned toward me. What was he doing here? How had he gotten here?

"Amber." Amari stepped toward me. "I'm going to walk toward you."

Why was he telling me that? That was when I realized that I shook like I might vibrate off into space and I was covered in blood. I lifted my hand. "I k-k-killed your mother, Amari." There was my stutter. It had been a good long time since it reared its head but there it was. I might not be able to form words in a second it was going to get so bad.

Anxiety driven all the way, I couldn't help it if I wanted to.

"I know. That's okay. I'm not upset with you. Hunter and Shane won't be upset with you. I'm just so fucking relieved we got here. Kelton." He looked over his shoulder at his cousin. When had he gotten there? "Tell the doctor to be ready. We're coming on board. He needs to take care of my wife."

Kelton nodded. "On it."

Amari turned his attention back to me. He did what he said he was going to and crossed to me before drawing me into his arms. I was disgusting. How could he even want to touch me? I put my head down on his shoulder. 'She d-d-did it again."

"Did what? Hurt you? Yes, it's... unbelievable to me. I spared her life. And she did this? I should have taken off her head. She was never warm, never a good mother. We had no relationship. I kept trying to figure out what to do with her. Never mind. Not important now."

No, he didn't understand. "I'm sure she k-k-killed the babies. She hit me with electricity. Again. I had decided to try, to believe there might be a w-w-way."

Amari pulled back to stare me straight in the face. "Babies? Are you pregnant, my love?"

I managed to nod ahead of the tears that spilled down my face. "I was."

"Do you know for sure that you lost them? You said plural right?"

I thought about it. "N-n-no."

"Then we go see. Come on." He picked me up into his arms like I wasn't capable of walking, since I might not have been, and carried me off the illegal shuttle I hoped I never saw again.

The med bay on the flagship of the Chen Empire fleet was nicer than the one we had on the ground. I'd met Doctor Woody once before. He was the private doctor to the Chen brothers and I guessed Amari got to keep him with him in this war.

"She's pregnant." Amari said as he walked us through the door. "And she has that condition I had you look up."

The doctor visibly winced. "Were you injured, Mrs. Chen?"

"It's Doctor now." I didn't know why I felt the need to correct him.

He smiled at me. "That's good. I was hoping they'd get you through the testing. That's wonderful Dr. Chen. Were you hurt?"

"I was hit with electricity. I got into a pretty bad fight."

He nodded. "Put her down, Master Chen."

Amari squeezed me tightly. "I'm not sure I can. I'm... I'm having trouble putting her down. Never mind. I'll do it."

The rest of the exam was a blur until the doctor put the screen on that would show the babies were there any babies to show. Or it would show no heartbeats at all.

But then there they were. Two heartbeats. I leaned forward as Doctor Woody grinned down at me. "They're doing just fine. Whatever happened... they hung on."

They hung on.

Amari pressed his cheek against mine, looking up. "That's them? They're okay?"

I nodded. "They're f-fine."

"Shit." He let out a long breath. Were his cheeks wet? I'd no sooner realized that than he'd wiped them away. "They're okay. That's good." He kissed my cheek. "I knew they'd be okay. And you're okay."

The doctor shook his head. "Well, she will be after I treat some of those bruises. We can't knock her out thanks to the pregnancy unless it's an absolute emergency. Then you're going to need to rest."

I laughed. "I just got finished resting. I have b-b-been c-c-concussed."

Amari sucked in a breath. "What?"

I snuggled closer to him. If he didn't care that I was

dirty and gross, then I wasn't going to complain. "Not so easy to t—t-talk right now."

He kissed my cheek. "That'll stop. We'll talk then. You're safe. They're safe. I might be able to breathe again someday. I'm running a war, and I haven't been this afraid in battle."

The doctor laughed. "I'll give you something if you want."

"I'm good." Amari nudged me. "He's known me since I was born."

That at least explained Amari's ease with him and the way that Doctor Woody got to tease Amari in a way I only saw his brothers do. The purple sash indicated he was Z like everyone else around my husbands. The thought brought me up short. "They k-killed Brenden."

Amari shook his head. "No, they didn't. The report that came to me was from Matt. Brenden lived. He took out two of her men. He did get hurt but help got there. He's okay."

I cried out, covering my mouth. "That's g-g-good. Thank you."

"You like Brenden?" He lifted his eyebrows.

"Not like I like you." There. I'd managed to say that without stuttering.

He smirked at me. "You just like me?"

I shook my head. "I love you like the air I breathe."

The teasing moment stopped. He cupped the side of my face, avoiding any bruises there. "Amber."

"All right, you two. Amari move. I'm going to fix up her face."

My husband didn't let go instantly but did eventually step back. "I assume they've told you the sex of the babies."

"No." I hadn't asked anything. Right now it was all about did they have hearts beating and were they going to survive the inhospitable environment that was my uterus. "What are they? I mean probably boys, right?"

He'd have that on the readout his med machine scanner gave him. "No. You, young lady, will be presenting the Chen Empire with the first girls born to the Chen family themselves since before the bombs went off."

Woody dropped that news like a bomb. I was in a family with two girls. That was considered huge. But my sister was, so far, having boys and the fact was that statistically we were all more likely to have boys in this universe where girls were so rare.

Amari's arms were back around me. "There will never be more protected or cherished children. That would have been true if they were boys, too. Which one of my brothers overachieved like this? Did they both get home regularly while I floated and battled in space?"

The doctor laughed, throwing his head back.

When I stopped grinning, I answered him. "All three of you have asked me some v-version of that of that question. Only Shane made it h-home, once."

"Once?" He kissed my cheek. "Comes home once and leaves you with twins. He always did like to do things in a big way. Used to try to show us up in school, too. I'm kidding. You know how happy I am right now? Do you know what you've given us? Something to hold onto you. Thank you, Amber. I don't know how we got lucky enough for any of this. You're going to be so happy and so safe."

I touched his cheek. "Is the war over?"

He held up three fingers. "They have one stronghold left. We kick them out of there and they're off of Earth. Then we just need to put them back into their black hole and make sure they never come back. My part is over in three days when we kick them out of there. Then I'll come home to you and we can rebuild." He touched my stomach. "Lots of happiness to look forward to."

"Look what you did, Dr. Chen." Woody winked. "You made him an optimist. I never thought I'd see the day. Now, move, Master Chen before I move you."

My husband grumbled but got out of the way.

I sat in the bathtub and let the warm water soak my troubles away. Amari had a bathtub connected to his room on this ship. I didn't have one back on Earth in our underground bunker. I was going to soak in this water as long as I could.

My husband walked in, closing the door behind him.

"How long?" I assumed he'd know what I asked him. How long did I have with him until he had to leave?

He took off his shirt. Something had banged him up; there were bruises there that were still healing. Maybe they were days old. He lifted his gaze to mine. "I have to bring you back, get our supplies, and leave. We have a number of hours together."

Amari followed with his pants, until he'd taken off all his clothing. I sat up, hoping I knew what he wanted, and he crawled into the tub behind me. "I haven't gotten in this thing the whole time. It's all about fast showers. But the men are silently managing things like they know I'm not separating from my wife right now, so I will soak with you unless you want to kick me out."

I shook my head. "In."

His big body took up a lot of space in the water, but as I leaned back against his chest, the water covered both of us. He kissed the top of my head, his arms coming around my body. "I heard from Blaze that you were already moving that Sienna woman when he got there. Good work. We still don't know why they want her, but the people who've been captured and rescued say the majority of the torture they're undergoing has to do with trying to get information on her. She is the most wanted woman in the galaxy as far as Evander is concerned so she can therefore never be given to them."

"I don't know that I could have protected her. I don't even know where we would have stashed her, but it was good Blaze got there."

He kissed my neck. "Things haven't been easy at home, have they? Sounds like there is a lot on your shoulders. I'm sorry."

"I'm sorry you're leading men into battle and covered in bruises. How did you get them?"

He was quiet for a second. "We ended up in hand-to-hand combat against some Evander Super Soldiers. The problem with them is when we beat them, and they are beatable if we overwhelm them with force, we're not sure what to do with them. We don't want to necessarily kill them. They're all under control by Evander and Rohan thinks some of them can be saved, rehabbed out of their mind control to think for themselves, but in the meantime, what to do. I got these bruises trying not to kill one of them. Unfortunately, that didn't work out for him."

My heart clenched. "I'm sorry."

"Me, too."

I turned in his arms so I could look at his face. He had his eyes closed, but he didn't look like he was going to sleep. More like he just wanted to shut out the world. I hated to say what I had to right then. "You can't really be okay with what I did to your mom. I meant to kill her. I was surprised that I did, but when I woke up, I knew exactly what had to happen."

He opened his dark eyes. "She's been dead to me for a long time. I'm not just saying that. You can believe me. She hurt you for years. I tried to spare her life but never wanted to see her again. I didn't want some tearstained forgiveness scene on her deathbed. I legitimately never wanted to see her again. I don't care that she's dead. I'm sorry it came to you having to do that and that you and my nieces had to suffer at her hands to get there. Fuck that. She almost took this from me. Again. That's not a mother. Maybe she was sick. I don't care. I'm glad to be rid of her. My father and uncles raised us."

I kissed him squarely on the lips, and he sighed against me. "I love you, Amari."

"Is it safe for me to make love to you? Okay for the baby?"

I nodded. "Should be. The things that can harm them come from me, not from you."

He brushed my hair off my face. "They're going to make it. I can feel it in my bones. They're with us now."

I crawled up his body. I didn't have the sense of things the way that my husbands did. I knew next to nothing about energy and feeling the universe. But I loved this man. I'd loved him when I shouldn't have, when a smart person would have let that feeling disappear, I hadn't. He was mine. He was meant to be mine, and I wanted to feel him inside of me one more time before I had to do without him for however long it was until he came home to me again.

I kissed his chin, his nose, his cheekbones. He shuddered against me. "How were you here when I needed you?"

"Coming back to get supplies." He kissed my neck, his

voice low, practically a whisper, even though we were alone. "Wanted to see you for just a few minutes. The call came over, asking if any ships had seen my mother's." He changed direction, kissing the other side of my neck. "Was just glad to be so close."

I kissed his mouth, turning around so I could lie flat on top of him. My breasts ached as my nipples hardened instantly.

Amari swiped his hands down my back, stopping at my ass where he massaged the skin. "Love that I can touch you. I wake up hard and needing you. I feel like a teenager again. Constantly grumpy and nothing to do but know that I am missing the fuck out of my wife."

I kissed his chest. "You're an ache. I never heard from you. I started to wonder if you vanished into space."

"I never wanted to risk you by communicating. Evander doesn't have to know where my wife is."

I reached between us, finding his hard cock. I smiled at the feel of him even as he flared his nostrils at my touch.

"You did miss me."

He nuzzled my neck. "So much. Don't touch me too long or I'm going to come in your hand instead of inside your sweet pussy."

I loved when he used words like that. Amari was so controlled most of the time. With me, he swore. With me, he suddenly spoke language not fit for business meetings. There was nothing sexier than Amari losing his control.

I let go of him but only so I could turn around. "Take me from behind."

"What?" I'd startled him. I wasn't usually demanding when it came to things like this. For so long, it had meant nothing but pain. Now, I wanted pleasure. I wanted all of it. And I wanted him to take me that way.

I looked over my shoulder. "Don't want to?"

"I want you however you want it. Scoot forward." We splashed water everywhere. That was okay. I'd clean it up later. I grabbed the other side of the tub, noticing that my knuckles had swollen. That was also something I'd deal with later.

For now, there was Amari and the sweet things he was doing to my back with his mouth. He kissed one shoulder blade and then the other. "You're so beautiful, Amber. You never cease to take my breath away."

"Amari." I choked on saying his name. "I love you."

"I love you, too."

He fit himself inside of me slowly. At this angle, he could go much deeper. I closed my eyes, a moan I'd never heard myself make before escaping from my lips.

"Like that?" Oh, how I loved how he whispered. "I want to give you so much pleasure."

After that his words seemed to make less and less sense. He spoke to me almost the entire time that his body loved mine. He wanted me, he loved me. I ate all of it up even as my brain shut down to simply absorb nothing but pleasure.

He found my clit and stroked it as he thrust inside of me. I leaned my head back, feeling the rub of his whiskers on my cheek, loving the bite of pain. I pressed my hips against him. In this position I couldn't move much, but I could squeeze him the way I wanted to.

Amari stopped talking, his words changing to sighs and moans. Soon, we were making them together. Every pass in and out of my body rubbed me in all the right spots. His hand moved, but only so he could squeeze my breasts. I held onto the side of the tub for dear life. I needed to come, wanted it.

Finally, as I squeezed him inside of me, it happened. I

lost myself in the pleasure. My body exploded and tears sprung from my eyes. I loved this man so much and it was still possible I could lose everything. Pleasure and sadness mixed together until I couldn't differentiate one from the other. He followed me into my strange oblivion, and if he found anything odd about it, he didn't indicate it. That was the thing about this man I adored, he understood big emotions and he never asked me to restrain them.

I panted, still holding onto the side of the bathtub. Reality would come back any second, but for now I had Amari, and I wasn't letting him go.

AMARI FELL asleep as the ship flew through space, heading back home where he would leave me and go do whatever had to be done to end this war. I didn't sleep. Knowing how little time we had together, I listened to him breathe. He slept deeply, his arms around me. It wasn't going to take us very long to get back. In fact, I'd be arriving just in time to have my next treatment, assuming there weren't emergencies happening that meant I couldn't have a med machine.

Amari said something unintelligible and shifted slightly. His dreams were not restful. I couldn't blame him. There was nothing peaceful happening right now. Plus, despite what he'd said about not being upset, there had to be a part of him where the fact that I'd killed his mother didn't sit well. I'd been okay with the idea that she had been gone. Mistrustful of it in some ways but comfortable with the fact that she'd vanished from my existence.

Now, I'd ended her life.

That was an entirely different thing. I touched my stomach. She'd carried my husbands like I now did these girls who I hoped I would actually get to meet. Her guards were loyal to her, all the way to their deaths. Brenden had fought for me. Yet, I didn't want to understand her—there was no way to really forgive, at least for me, what she'd done.

I hadn't wanted to kill her. I was a doctor. I saved lives. Now, I'd taken one, and I wasn't fooling myself, I'd woken up intending to do it.

"Amber," Amari spoke my name. I rolled slightly to look at him. He still slept. He'd warned me the first time we shared a bed to sleep that he was restless but then with me he'd been silent and still.

I kissed his chest. "Rest, my love. You are safe. You are well."

He did seem to settle. We stayed like that until I felt the telltale feeling in my ears that said we were landing soon. The ship would slowly start to alter its gravity to meet Earth's. It would be gentle unless we encountered some reason to descend faster.

They were going to need Master Chen soon. I brushed his hair out of his face. "Amari."

He didn't stir, so I did it again, kissing his cheek. "Amari, time to wake up."

His eyes opened this time. "Already?"

"Yes. Unfortunately. I feel the descent." I pointed to my ears. "I'm sensitive to it."

"You're right, I feel it, too." He stretched his arms over his head. "Did you sleep?"

I shook my head. "Didn't want to. I wanted every minute I could have to be awake ones."

His face fell. "You should have woken me. We could have talked."

"No." I kissed his other cheek. "I was glad you were resting. You needed it, as brief a time as it was."

The engines rumbled, but neither of us moved to get up.

He ran his fingers through my hair. "What should we do to celebrate when I get back?"

"There isn't going to be much room for celebrating. The house is gone."

He blinked. "It's gone?"

"Bombed. We'll have to find homes for all of those people, start to fix things up. The water is still running. I check on it every day and..."

Amari tugged me to him. "Thank you."

"No, it's nothing. Two minutes a day."

He shook his head. "I don't mean for the water although, yes, thank you for that. No, thank you for keeping our home safe. I know it's you. Even if you don't know it."

A ding sounded in the room, and a voice I didn't know spoke. "Master Chen, sorry to disturb you, but we're here."

"I'm up, Donald. We'll be out in a minute."

"Yes, sir." The ding repeated, indicating the person was gone from the speaker.

Don't go, Amari. That was on the tip of my tongue, but of course I didn't say it. I could think it, though. I could be desperate and weak and sad in my thoughts. No one ever had to know them. I smiled at him instead. "Be as safe as you can and come back. I'm going to need your help in decorating a new house for us."

He snorted. "That is going to be all you."

Amari never had to know just how close I'd come to begging him to stay. He didn't need to carry that into battle.

━━

AMARI

A group of fifteen Z Warriors waited as we exited the ship. It took me a second to realize they weren't here to greet me. No, my wife's guards swarmed her as she exited, each one of them bowing before they hugged her. *They hugged her?*

This was a new occurrence in the history of the Z and the Chen family. They didn't hug us. Sometimes the chosen few laughed with us. Hugging? Brenden stood in the center, his head bowed, as she spoke to him, her hand on his shoulder.

"No, you saved me. I was there. There is nothing to apologize for. Stop it. You didn't fail."

I wanted her hand off of his arm. I stayed silent, stilling my body, breathing. I'd wanted her to bond to her Z. What was the conversation Hunter and I had about it? Was that a million years ago? No, maybe only months.

She needed them to be safe, and traditionally, the Chen wife did get close to her guards. In my mother's case, too close. We'd needed her to stop being afraid of them, and we'd gone out of our way to assign Brenden to lead the group because she'd like him.

He'd picked the other fourteen.

This was what we wanted.

Only, I didn't get to stay here with them right now. I didn't get to have her hugs and her touches and her warmth. I had to only remember it to keep me warm in the upcoming days.

I was selfish, always had been. I cared about my people, but the truth was when it came to Amber, I only wanted to share her with my brothers.

"Amber." I put out my hand, and to my relief she turned

instantly to my voice. Her hand came down in mine. "I want to get you settled before I have to go."

She kissed my arm. That was better. Her snuggles were for me. She didn't treat the Z like that. There was a different warmth for me than she had for them. She was mine.

"Thank you for taking care of her, gentlemen. Brenden, you get a special commendation. You're moving up in rank."

He shook his head before bowing it. "I cannot accept that, Master Chen. To care for the Chen wife is my honor."

That was the right answer. I did like the kid. I just wanted to kill him for having some of my wife's constant attention when I got to have so little of it. "Regardless, the rank up is yours. For all of you, actually."

She squeezed my arm as we walked together. "That is so nice of you. They're really wonderful men."

"Amber, do me a favor." I stopped walking and took her soft cheeks in my hands. "Until I am back with you where I can let my gaze travel over you several times a day and feel your curves against me at night, your lips on mine, don't hug them."

Her breath quickened. "Amari... you can't possibly think that..."

I stopped her with a shake of my head. "No, I don't. But we had two years apart and now this time, and I am crazed. I'll admit it. One time with you in a matter of hours is not going to sate my need for you. I don't think I will emerge from your sweetness for years. I know that's not realistic, but I think you should expect to suddenly find me near you all the time when I get back to the point that you'll wonder if I've attached myself to your leg."

Her smile was huge. "Promise?"

I groaned. "Woman, you should tell me to back off."

"That isn't what I want." She sighed. "I have to go to the med machine. I hate it but that's where I have to go."

I touched her stomach. There were two lives in there. As soon as this time was over, she was going to sit with her feet up. She could direct people from the ease of her chair.

The central location of the empire had been decimated. I wouldn't have recognized it if I'd stumbled upon it unknowingly. Sometime in the not too distant future, I would get to mourn what had happened here. I would dwell on the lives lost. I would think about all that Evander destroyed, and I would let myself, in privacy, weep for it all. I wouldn't even mind if Amber saw. She'd almost caught me tear up over the babies the day before in the med bay.

I didn't think she'd think less of me for it.

The med bay was busy, filled with people waiting to be seen. Some of them doubled over in pain. Amber stiffened before she jumped into action.

"Dr. Chen," a woman I'd known since birth called out to her, extending her arms. She was covered in blood. For years, she'd worked in the main house, cleaning the public wings. What happened to her?

Amber was by her side. "Mary, what happened?"

"Oh, Amber, it was awful. The oven blew up."

My wife's eyes widened. "It blew up? Let's look at you."

Two things struck me at once. One, my people were comfortable enough with my wife that they called her by her first name. Well, she'd called her Dr. Chen first but they came to informality rather quickly. And Amber knew this woman instantly.

A lot had changed in my months away. There was a time the people rejected Amber, thanks to my mother. Everything altered in such a short period of time.

My wife helped Mary to her feet and brought her to the med machine.

Ari spun around from where he operated on a patient's arm outside of the machine. "That one is for you, Amber. We saved it for you. You need the treatment." He pointed to it. "Don't put Mary in that."

Amber shot bullets at Ari from her gaze. "I can't take other people's spots."

"You're not being a prima donna, Amber. You have two people inside of you who need you to do just that. So don't complain. Mary is not at death's door. I'll get to her in a second."

"Ari, the only reason I've been able to do the treatments was we were relatively clear in here."

He pointed at the machine. "Don't argue with me. Get in. I uploaded your tablet. You should be able to read things while you're in there since you have to stay awake."

"They're girls." I suspected he knew that and just hadn't told Amber yet.

He grinned at her. "I see Woody let you know. Yes, they're girls. And they're going to have a shot at life. This is the Chen Empire. You're Amber Chen. Everyone here wants those babies."

"You're pregnant," Mary gasped. "Get in the machine."

I walked over to her. "I'll sit with you, Mary, until it's your turn."

She gasped. "Master Chen, I didn't see you there."

"Come on." I winked at Amber.

We both knew I wouldn't see her again on this trip. I'd have to go while she was still inside the machine. But I would see her soon. That much I'd promised not just to her, but to me.

I was coming home. We were going to fucking rebuild.

Amber, my brothers, those baby girls. They were all going to have a future. The whole Chen Empire would rise again. I'd carry them all on my shoulders if need be.

———

AMBER

I read through the letters Hunter had written me and tried not to focus on the fact Amari must have left. I wiped away a tear. Being in the med machine was truly terrible awake. I hated it asleep, but if I suffered from any kind of claustrophobia, this would have been unbearable.

Finally, I got to Hunter's last message, which was problematic as I was about to lose the one thing I'd done to distract myself since getting inside of this thing.

I had to stop whining. I was having babies. I had to keep them safe inside of me. The people around me moved mountains for me even in the midst of this war to keep me safe. This was officially the last time I would think about how uncomfortable I was.

There. Done.

I opened Hunter's last letter.

Amber,

I was getting worried I hadn't heard from you so I reached out to Ari. He let me know what happened, and I am so glad my brother arrived right on time. I keep not being there for you. I'll make it up with a lifetime of being right under your nose to help with anything you ever need. Anyway, I sat up obsessing over the fact that you got taken and hurt by Mother. Please don't worry about how that ended up. Ari told me the whole story.

She wasn't okay. If it was her versus you... In the end, you're here and I couldn't be more relieved and happy about that. Please see below what I did. It's a design I came up with at three am. Maybe it'll help with the babies.

I love you,

H

I stared at the design he'd made. It was some kind of machine, and the best I could understand it, he'd designed it to be strapped to my abdomen. It would perform the procedure constantly. Would that work?

I banged on the top of the machine, and Ari came over to stare down at me.

I held up my tablet and then sent the design to his. He stared at it and then at me. Ari held up one finger. Okay. He'd be back.

I started typing, which was awkward, but I did it.

Hunter,

Sorry it's been so long. Between the concussion and the abduction I couldn't communicate this way. I love you. Thank you for the design. Ari is looking into it now. I think. I'm not really sure what he's doing. I'm in the med machine right now.

I wish I had more to share with you, but I kind of think some experiences are better off keeping to myself. You guys seem to feel that way, too. Like things we're doing here during this time are only for this time and when we talk or are together, we don't dwell on it a lot. I don't know if that's a good thing or a bad thing, but it seems to be what we're doing.

The house is gone. I don't mean the summer house. I mean the main house. Evander bombed it. So we'll need a new house. Don't stay up all night dwelling, but if you have any free time and want to design... maybe start with that? Then our summer home. I'm not demanding or anything, right?

The babies are girls.

I love you.

A

I didn't know if the tablet would call from inside the machine but I hit the button anyway and a second later Shane appeared. He grinned at me.

"You look funny, Amber. I heard what happened from Hunter. He sent me a note. You okay?" His smile faded as he talked. "I can't talk long. But you okay?"

"I'm okay." I just wanted to hear his voice. "They're girls, Shane. You gave me two baby girls to carry. Thank you for that."

His mouth dropped open. "Girls. I... Shit, I have to go. Take care of yourself and those girls. I'll be back to take care of all of you soon. I love you."

The tablet disconnected. Maybe things were starting right then. Could the battles have begun so fast? I should have made Amari show me on a map where everything was happening. Or maybe it was better I didn't know.

I had to breathe. I closed my eyes. Now would have been a great time to practice that meditating. It wasn't the same as getting to cuddle with my guys while I did it, but I'd close my eyes and seek calm. I breathed and tried to imagine Hunter's voice telling me to focus.

I concentrated on how my body felt. Usually, this was where I fell apart, but today it came easily. I could feel my feet, my hands, I could feel the blood rushing through my body. Minutes passed. Or maybe it was longer. I didn't feel like I needed to open my eyes or rush to anything.

There was just the air in my lungs and my heart beat. At some point, if Hunter was doing this with me, he'd tell me to focus on a problem, to send it out to the energy in the universe, and see what came back.

I tried to do that. Since the girls were fine so far, I wasn't having problems except for worrying about my husbands. There was nothing I could do to fix my worry about them except try to send them loving energy and hope it somehow reached them. This was really loopy for me. I didn't go around doing things like sending out loving energy. But that was what I concentrated on doing.

It couldn't hurt.

A jolt passed through me. I must really have been thinking about them because it did feel like Hunter was right there with me, as though he caressed me with his hand. I just knew it was him. I shook my head and opened my eyes.

Maybe I'd fallen asleep and imagined him.

Ari opened the top. "Hey, look who woke up. Was just going to wake you."

"I wasn't really sleeping. Maybe I was at the end there. Meditating. Was that six hours?"

Ari nodded. "It was and the good news, if you can endure a little more discomfort today, then we can make it so you don't have to do that again."

Hunter's design? "What are you thinking?"

"He made it so it would sit on your abdomen. That made me nervous. What if it moves? So I brought Lewis in on it..." The door opened, interrupting Ari's statement.

As though he'd been called, Lewis strode in. "Did you tell her?"

"I was just in the middle of it. Lewis is going to implant the device inside of you. Right where it needs to go with a direction to turn on once a day."

They were going to what? There were lots of implanted devices that did this. Diana had one. Why didn't we consider this earlier?

"Will it be safe for the babies?"

Lewis grinned. "Perfectly. Come on. Calm moment. We're going to do it right now. By tonight, you'll know the babies are as safe as we can make them."

"There's still risk. There was even doing it the way we're doing it. Your body, as you know, it's not a real safe zone for pregnancies. Your sister has major issues. But there are two healthy Sandler boys now, so let's do this." Ari nodded like he wanted me to agree.

Hunter designed this. There was something just right about his idea being what saved them. I sent him some love and a second later, that same feeling came back. I rubbed my arms, wishing I could run around in it.

"You okay?" Ari tilted his head as he looked at me.

I nodded. "You wouldn't believe me if I told you. Can you knock me out?"

Lewis shook his head. "They used to knock pregnant women out with the med machine drugs. I understand from Dane he had Melissa out several times when they had Diana inside of her. But we don't do that now. There is the possibility of it traveling through the placenta."

He was giving me a history lesson I didn't need, but since I'd asked the question as though I didn't do this as a profession, I listened like a lay person. It was nice to have him talk to me like this, it was nice to just be the patient.

"In other words, I will do this with you awake, but you won't feel it."

"You have it made?"

Lewis grinned. "Diana made it from the design using the replicators."

Then there was no need to continue on like this. "Let's do this thing."

I settled on the table and decided to focus on sending out more of that energy. I sent it to Shane. To Amari. It took a little longer but Amari's came back, rushing over me. I smiled. He was so much strength whereas Hunter had been surety. Shane was last. It was pure adoration. I smiled. I might have been crazy, but it felt fantastic.

I'd go with it.

Diana bounced Allie on her knee. The little girl was eighteen months old now. How had so much time passed? Paloma nursed Aaron in the chair in the corner, and across the room, which really wasn't that far considering how small it was, Waverly nursed Mason. Ben and Helene played on the floor with Emerson who was remarkably ahead for his age. He was much younger than they were and yet he kept up.

I pointed at him. "Is it the Super Soldier genes?"

"It might be." Waverly smiled. "I try not to dwell on it. I try not to dwell on a lot of things."

Diana nodded. "In constant denial."

We all had that in common. All of us sitting here while the people we loved battled and fought. "I'd suggest we all have a drink but the only one here who can do that is Diana."

She grinned. "And I don't drink alcohol. Besides, it's non-essential. Where would you get it?"

I had a feeling if I asked Brenden I could pretty much have what I wanted. Still, there wasn't a point. Diana sat forward. "You just lay there while they cut you open?"

"I did. There wasn't pain. Thank you for your help." I touched her arm.

She shook her head. "This whole time you've been doing so much around here, keeping us all safe when there is no safety, making this situation as palatable as it could be. Never complaining. Staying up all night. I don't always talk because sometimes I can't, but I always notice." She sighed. "You and I share that, Amber. I'm certainly going on right now." She laughed. Sometimes Diana was quirky in the best possible way. "I was so glad to finally be able to help you."

"You do help me. You all do. You're here. I think about it sometimes, how you all ended up here. You could have waited out this mess anywhere in the universe, some outpost somewhere, but you all stayed here. I loved having people here. Thank you."

Paloma rolled her eyes. "This is the center here. This is Earth. Our families come through here, once in a blue moon, but they do. There's nowhere to go if we don't win. Nowhere in the universe would be safe. Not even across that black hole. Evander already ruined over there. We stay here, we stay with family, we do this together." She pointed at me. "And you are going to need lots of family when the babies come. Plural. Crazy."

I chewed on my lip. "By then, this should be over. You guys will be back on The Farm."

Paloma waved her hand. "I'll be back when those babies come. Like I'd let my baby sister have her first babies without me there."

Diana and Waverly caught each other's eyes. It was Diana who spoke. "We'll be there for you, too."

I smiled. It was so good to have friends and family. Everything had exploded but not this.

I woke to knocking on the door. I was tired, ridiculously so, and moving slower than usual. I managed to get to the door. My voice didn't want to work, I had to clear it several times. "Brenden? What's up?"

No one had pinged me. It couldn't be medical.

"Battle is over, Dr. Chen." He pulled me into a hug. "We have news that it's over. We won. Our people are starting to come back."

I threw my arms around him, and after he stiffened, he laughed. "I don't think Master Chen liked you hugging us." He stepped back. "Although totally appropriate right now. I'm told that several ships have chased what remains of Evander, and they're going to push them through the black hole."

I caught my breath. "That has to be my husbands. No way would they leave it undone."

"I agree. Whoever is doing it, they're with them for sure. Even then it shouldn't be too long."

A wave of nausea hit me. "Sorry, Brenden, I have to

excuse myself. This is great news. Just... some of my pregnancy symptoms are getting worse by the day."

He stepped back, his eyes wide. "Let me know if you need anything."

Only time was going to fix this, but having my three guys back would go a long way to making this a lot more manageable.

We'd won. Well, they'd won. I'd sort of tried to help and made things more difficult for Amari in the process. Still, it was over. Evander Corporation would be leaving our skies forever.

Joy didn't flee, even through the puke.

———

I stayed back, standing in the corner of the shuttle area, and watched as spaceship after spaceship reunited families. There were some injured, mostly from one explosion that happened toward the end of the last battle, but for the most part we weren't overrun in the med area.

I'd gotten to know the people who'd stayed here during the war, but seeing them with their loved ones I didn't know made me smile. They had families and they were coming back. I sighed. The death notices were coming in, too. This hadn't been a casualty free endeavor. There were some people who would never recover from who they'd lost in these battles.

I blamed Evander. I always would.

I sipped my water and watched. There was no news from my husbands, and it had been confirmed, by Diana, that they'd gone off with a collection of Super Soldiers and Melissa Alexander's group to chase Evander back through the black hole.

Then it looked like someone was going to close that hole, rendering it impossible for them to ever come back here. It would also block those who sought refuge from them. I had a lot of mixed feelings on this subject. For now, all I wanted were my husbands back.

Jackson jumped out of a ship, followed by Damian. My heart rate kicked up. These were my friends—family, really —husbands returning. Jackson to Waverly, he'd still not met Mason. Damian to Diana. I knew how much of her heart that man held. Jackson nodded at Damian and patted him on the back. They both smiled.

"Jackson," Waverly yelled. When had she gotten here? He whirled around. I didn't try to stop the tears that came from my eyes as I silently witnessed this moment. I doubted they'd care. People surrounded us all, and for a second, I wanted to live vicariously through their happiness.

Jackson picked her up in his arms, and he kissed her like he needed her to survive. Waverly was a tall woman, but Jackson held her like she was tiny.

Damian laughed and kept walking, only to have his wife throw her arms around his neck. He whirled her around, utter delight crossing his features before he dipped her down to kiss her.

I let out a long breath.

I touched my ear, tapping it to reach Ari, who was in the med bay. "Jackson's back."

"For real?" He made a whooping sound. "On my way."

In the end, who we loved and what we did with the time we were allotted in life was really all that mattered. I was so glad this time was ending.

Canyon. Rohan. Sterling. Cash. Judge. All four Sandler brothers together. Slowly but surely, my sister and my friends' family units reformed over the next days.

But still nothing from mine. Not even a communication. I washed my hands, having just delivered a baby from a Z Warrior's wife, and tried not to dwell on that. Melissa Alexander and her husbands weren't back yet either and neither had half the Z who had gone to fight. Everyone confirmed what we'd heard from the others, it wasn't quite over until Evander went through that black hole.

I closed my eyes and sent them energy. The tingles came back. I loved how that went, how that felt. It was usually all three of them simultaneously now. I might have been crazy, but it was a happy crazy.

And that was my medical definition for it...

"Sister." Paloma hopped up on the med table to stare at me. "Where have you been?"

I blinked. "When?"

"For the last week. Where have you been?"

I pointed at the floor. "Mostly here."

"Well, I have been looking for you."

She was in an odd mood. It took a second for me to recognize it as giddiness. My sister was truly happy and relaxed for the first time in... I didn't know how long.

"For the last week?" I closed my tablet. I'd read about Martian measles another time. I doubted the man in the med machine had them. He'd probably eaten some bad mushrooms in one of the celebrations going on. People were looking for ways to relax.

She waved her hand. "Why haven't you come by?"

"Because you are reuniting with your family and I thought you might like some privacy to do so." The Sandler crew had made quite the scene when they'd landed, each of them yelling at the other in their quest to get to Paloma faster. She hadn't been in her rooms, having taken the children for a walk. Oh, how that had exploded into a frenzy. I'd found her and brought her home.

She squeezed my arm. "You're sweet. But you're coming by tonight. I'm hosting a family dinner."

Like the ones she'd had on The Farm? I'd loved them, but I was absolutely not in the mood. "I think I'm going to pass." I hugged her. "I'm not in a group gathering mood."

"Oh, come on. You know you want to come. Everyone will miss you if you're not there."

I sighed. "Paloma, I am so happy for you that your husbands are home. I love them. They really are my brothers. They've been nothing but good to me all these years. When Quinn came home to be there for you before he had to leave, I was so... ecstatic. I am excited that Diana's husbands are home and back to fixing the world. They are incredible men. I am over the moon that Waverly's loves have returned and they're in baby bliss. You're in baby bliss." I touched my chest. "My loves aren't back. I'm pregnant, but I've had no baby bliss. Try to imagine how you'd be feeling right now if your people weren't here yet."

Her smile fell. "I love you, Amber. I think it would be good for you to get out, see people who care about you, and stop being in your room alone every night, hoping your husbands will appear. When they get back they will find you. In my rooms if you're still there. I can't imagine any of them letting a hallway and a half keep them from seeing you."

My sister meant well. "Paloma..."

"If you don't come, Ben will cry."

I gasped. "What?"

"Ben will cry. And then I have to tell you, I know he's

too little, but Aaron is already so attached to Ben that he'll cry too. If they're crying, Helene is going to cry. Emerson doesn't cry much. But he'll get all red in the face, which is rather hard to do with his complexion, but I've seen it. Then they'll all be a mess and that'll all be your fault because you didn't come."

I pointed at her, narrowing my eyes. "That is an utterly horrible manipulation. Ooh. I saw what you did right there. I know how you're playing me."

She put her hands on her hips. "Did it work?"

"Yes. How can I stay home now thinking of Ben crying?"

She pointed at me. "You need to spend more time with us so you have less of a favorite. I'm not going to have a favorite when it comes to your daughters."

I glared at her. "Aaron doesn't yet have a personality. I love him. I delivered him. I feel very close to him. But he doesn't even really open his eyes."

She leaned forward. "You'd know his personality if you hung around a little bit more."

My sister was out of her mind. She'd cross the galaxy to save me. But she could drive me crazy, and she knew how to get under my skin, particularly if she thought it was for my own good. "I'll come for a little while."

Her smile was huge. "Great."

I'd totally been manipulated. Her Sandler husbands had nothing on her.

———

The party was in full swing when I got there. Paloma could call it a family dinner all she wanted, but tonight it was a party. Loud, happy voices carried down the hallway. The

Farm was downright luxurious compared to how we lived now. I hadn't heard anyone complain. We were all just waiting on news that Evander was back where they belonged. Then the rebuilding could start.

I didn't even know, probably because I didn't want to know, where my sister intended to live after this. Would her family go back to The Farm? Back to Sandler space? Stay here? I was going to miss the heck out of her if it wasn't here and that was why I didn't ask.

Manipulation or no manipulation.

I spotted my nephew Ben as soon as I arrived. He smiled at me, and I picked him up before I wondered if I should do that. I needed to be careful of the babies. I set him down and knelt down instead. "How is my favorite Benjamin?"

"Everyone is being loud tonight."

I looked around. They were. There was a lot of alcohol being passed around. My sister held the baby and sipped water. Diana and Waverly didn't seem to be drinking either. But the men? Yes, they were drinking.

"Amber." Clay knelt with me. "I'm so glad to see you. How are you? I heard the big news."

I stood to greet him, and he rose as well. "Thanks. Paloma's excited."

"Oh, I didn't hear it from Paloma. I heard it from Shane."

My heart flipped over. "You talked to Shane about it?"

Keith came over, leaning on Clay. "He talked about little else the last month. Great guy. Hugely helpful. I was sorry to lose him back to the Z ships at the end. And it sucks for him because he ended up still out there when he could have come home with us."

Clay shook his head. "Shane was never going to not go with the Z. He's Captain Z."

Brenden and Matt stayed in the hallway tonight, declining to come in. That was probably smart. I couldn't imagine them in here right now.

Rohan walked over joining us. "I heard it from Hunter."

Tommy laughed from across the room. "Well, you can all kiss my ass because I heard it from Amari himself. Tommy, do you have those numbers on the ships we took down? Thanks. Amber's having twins."

I couldn't help my smile. I hadn't seen them to have these moments, but they were clearly excited. That made me warm inside.

Tommy walked over. "You saved her and my son. Thank you."

I tapped his arm. "She says I'm favoring Ben."

Quinn handed me a glass of water. "I told her that would get your goat. That's the expression, right? It got you here. She knew you wouldn't want to tonight, but you needed a good home cooked meal and to let us all fawn all over you."

"What's with the animal expressions? The goat. The fawn?" I loved poking at Quinn.

He grinned. "We have two children now. I'm working on being relatable."

The door opened and Diana squealed. It was a funny sound that I wasn't used to from her, but in the next second she had her arms around her mother. Melissa Alexander stood in the doorway, embracing her daughter. I caught my breath.

Did Melissa being back mean that...

Melissa pulled back from Diana. "Is Amber here? Yes, there you are." She put out her hand. "Come with me."

She wanted me? Why? Still, I stepped away from the crowd and walked toward her. I wasn't sure I'd ever deny Melissa anything. She'd been such a powerhouse of a person when I was growing up.

I took her hand, and she squeezed it.

There were moments in life when I just knew someone was going to tell me something I didn't want to hear. When my mother came into my bedroom on Mars Station and told me we had to leave immediately because they were sending off my sister. When my mother-in-law came into my bedroom after my disastrous wedding night. When Dane had figured out what caused me so much pain in my uterus.

And now.

Still, I let her lead me into the hall. Paloma grabbed my free hand and didn't let go. She followed me out, squeezing my fingers. Whatever was going to happen, she didn't leave me alone.

The Z Warriors filled the hall. Brenden had his arms crossed over his chest, meeting my eyes with lowered lids. The others didn't look at me.

Kelton, my husbands' cousin who ran things when they weren't here, stood in the center. His eyes were red rimmed.

Okay. The buildup of this was too much. I dropped Melissa's hand.

"Tell me." I didn't speak to her. I spoke to Kelton. They were the Z. They were here to deliver this message. I was going to let them do it.

I didn't want to remember the sound of Melissa's voice speaking the words I knew were about to come. I didn't want to hear them again every time she spoke from now on.

Kelton bowed his head. "We chased Evander to the black hole."

"And?" They weren't all standing here to tell me that.

"They had a ship hidden in the hole. I've never seen anything like it. It was... practically invisible. Then it popped into existence as though it had always been there. That was tech the likes of which I have never seen. The battle was hard. They spit a substance into space. It was gray, it clogged up our radar, all of our systems went askew. No one could see anything. It was like firing into... a pot of stew. There were things everywhere and no one knew what to shoot at."

I swallowed. "And?"

Paloma hadn't let go of my hand. She squeezed me tighter. I didn't know if I liked that she did that or if I wanted her to stop touching me immediately. Touch might be too much. I... I didn't know.

Kelton continued. "Hunter figured it out. How to clear the stuff. He backtracked the engines, got them to shoot out particles that... well, it was brilliant."

"Of course it was." This was Hunter. "And he's dead. That's what you're going to tell me. We don't need this build up. Hunter is dead. Shane is dead. Amari is dead. In this battle where no one could see that Hunter solved, they still ended up dead."

I shouted. I could practically hear my also dead mother-in-law in my head. Chen wives don't scream at the Z. Well, this one did. This one did when they came to tell her that the loves of her life, who she'd had so little happy times with, who were supposed to be the fathers of her children—two of which she carried in her stomach—were dead.

Kelton dropped his head further. "The disguised ship fired and fired and fired. It tore the ships up. Then it took off to the Dark Planets. We found debris. Floating bodies. That is all that remains of the flag ship."

I didn't cry. That was funny. I wept so easily at things. I

was a constant crier, and yet I had no tears. "You found their bodies in space? Whatever was left of them?"

He shook his head. "Not of your husbands, no. I believe there was nothing left to find."

"Who did you find?" Why did I ask that? I didn't even know.

Kelton lifted his eyes. "Woody. Josiah. Others I'm not sure that you knew."

That was enough. They were my husbands' guards. Their doctor. There couldn't be a doubt. Wherever those men had been, my husbands were.

Melissa shook next to me. I could suddenly feel her vibrations through the air. She was exhausted. They'd flown all night to get here to tell me. All of these people had been in that battle and lived.

Amari. Hunter. Shane. They hadn't.

I lifted my head. "This was hard to tell me." My voice shook but no tears came. Still not a drop. "Thank you for delivering it so quickly."

"Mrs. Chen." Kelton lowered his head again.

I didn't correct him. Why bother? I didn't really care that I was a doctor. What did it matter? Brenden lifted his lids as though my failure to correct surprised him, but he didn't say anything. Everyone waited for me to speak again.

"I don't know if you gentlemen have heard but..." My mouth didn't want to work. "B-b-but." Damn it. Paloma pulled me against her, our sides touching. I had to get through this. "I'm going to have twin girls in about seven months. Master Shane visited and well, there will be babies. Maybe. I'm a very high r-r-risk pregnancy, which the Chens knew."

Paloma kissed my cheek. "You don't have to do this now."

"I d-do." I stepped away from her. I loved her, but I couldn't be babied, not when I had to do this. "I will do everything in my power to have them."

All the Z shifted, their heads rising for seconds at a time. Some of them had tears in their eyes.

"Amber." Melissa sobbed and C.J. was suddenly there to put his arms around her. When had her husbands arrived?

I met Kelton's gaze. "They're the heirs, r-r-right? Does it matter that they're girls?" I had never asked anyone this. If I was simply having them to give them over to the highest bidder then I would disappear in the middle of the night with them immediately. They were the Chen heirs. Their father and uncles would have seen to it if they lived.

Kelton nodded. "There is no rule that a woman can't rule the Empire or that she can't lead up the Z. Whichever one of them is born first will have that title. And her sister will have the roles of Hunter and Shane. Treasured, essential."

"Then hold this place for them. We're going to fix it. There will be something for them to inherit when they come of age." I pointed at Brenden. "You'll teach them how to be Z. That's on you."

He stepped toward me. "Amber... sorry, Dr. Chen. There are better people for that role."

"No, by then it'll be you." I walked away. I was going to lose it. My hands shook, and I would not leave myself open to be discussed by the Z for the rest of my life for the way that I'd lost it now. My daughters had to rule here, they had to live here, they had to have a life. That meant that I would survive this. I would stay here in this place I once hated, and I would make this work.

I owed it to Amari. To Hunter. To Shane.

I would not run again. Not even from their deaths.

———

I made it to my room and then threw myself down on the bed. My sister hadn't chased me, and I appreciated that. She probably had to go deliver the news to the room. I curled my knees to my chest. I didn't have a baby bump yet. No one could have told I was pregnant. And yet the heartbeats inside of me were what I had to focus on.

From this moment forward and always.

I hadn't had happiness long. That was my own fault. I'd thrown it away without fighting for it. If I'd been then who I was now, I'd have put my finger in my husbands' faces at a meal in front of their mother and demanded they make the beatings stop or I was leaving. Then maybe we'd have understood each other. Then, maybe I wouldn't have been left with nothing but regret.

No, it wasn't nothing but regret. I didn't get a happy ending. Fine. Who really did in this universe? Even the happy couples in Paloma's rooms suffered. We'd all just endured war.

A knock sounded. "Dr. Chen." It was Brenden. "Matt and I are here. We're not leaving. We're not going to bother you, but we are here."

I closed my eyes. Amari really had known who to assign me. The first tear struck, and I wiped it away. I had to think. I had to focus.

There would be happiness for the girls. There would be the future their father and uncles died for. Exploded in space.

I had to calm down before I made myself sick. I sat up. I

had to breathe. I knew how to do that. I could meditate. I'd do it every damn day.

I closed my eyes. I breathed in through my nose and out my mouth. That was all I let myself do. I breathed. It was hard, but I did it. Eventually, when my hands tingled, I knew it was time to focus. This was when I'd have sent my love out to my husbands. They weren't around to receive it anymore, but I did it anyway. Why not? I could send love out to the dead.

I loved them.

The feeling brushed over me. Shane first. Then Amari. Finally Hunter. What? That wasn't possible. Of course, none of this was very likely to begin with. I'd probably always made up feeling their presences in my mind.

I was looking for what couldn't be now.

I pushed back with my grief, with my sadness, with the gaping ache they'd left me with.

It was as though Shane's hand touched my back. My eyes flew open. If I accepted the idea that I wasn't crazy, then somehow I was feeling them. In the meditative state, I could touch them. They responded to me. They were incredibly powerful Z. They practically bent the air when they fought. Why wasn't it possible?

They vibrated when they meditated. They'd been sure I had a connection like they did.

I'd sent love out, and I'd gotten it back.

And I didn't believe in ghosts.

My husbands weren't dead.

I STEPPED out of my bedroom. Brenden and Matt both jumped to their feet.

"Dr. Chen?" Brenden asked. "Is there something we can do for you?"

I nodded at them. "I need to speak to the Z. To Kelton. He's in charge now? I'm going to speak to them, now. Please. By the water." I wanted to see it, to hear the sound of it running.

Brenden nodded. "We'll get them for you. And Dr. Chen, you're in charge. You will be until the girls are old enough. That'll be when they're eighteen."

I couldn't even feel them yet and we already planned for them to be eighteen. Well, I was going to get back their father and their uncles. I didn't have the slightest interest in leading. Amari was born for it, and he did it well. I'd get him back here to do it.

In the meantime, I nodded. I walked slowly to the water area, staring up at the waterfall. I put my hand in it to feel the cool water.

"Amber?" Melissa said my name, and I turned around

to see her standing there next to my sister, Diana, and Waverly. They'd all come looking for me?

I put my hands on my hips. "I'm going to need you to believe me."

Paloma took me in her arms. "About what?"

"About something that is going to seem so unbelievable I wouldn't believe me. I need you... to extend me the benefit of the doubt beyond that which is reasonable."

My sister furrowed her brow. "Why are you out? You should be lying down."

"No." I shook my head. "I'm right where I need to be."

The Z entered the room, most of them with their heads down. This would go one of two ways. Either they would go along with this, or I was going to steal a ship and somehow find them myself. I had one path now, and it was clear to me.

When I spoke, it was to Kelton. "Months ago, Hunter taught me how to meditate. I'd never given much thought to the act before then. Breathing in. Breathing out. Whatever. But it was different with them. They could do things during meditation I'd never seen. It almost seemed like their whole bodies vibrated."

Kelton nodded. "We can all manipulate energy. My cousins could do it better than most. I can do it a bit. All the Z can do it. Amazing you could see it. Most lay people can't."

"Yes, that was what Hunter said, too. He encouraged me to meditate." I had to get through the background information of this. "I didn't, but then after a while I did. It was very strange, and at first I thought I imagined it, but more and more I realized I didn't. I can feel them when I meditate. I send them love and energy. They send it back."

I turned my attention to my friends. "I realize this has to

sound out there. But think of all the other things we do and where we go and how odd those things can seem to outsiders. The Zansi Warriors can do things that have over the years blown my mind and terrified me. I have come to respect the time and devotion of it. I may never fully understand it myself and that's fine. I recognize that there's a long, strong history here."

I really hadn't meant to go on this tangent, but now that I was doing it I might as well continue. "A proud, long history of things that are almost... unbelievable. The Z care about the Chens to a point of almost spiritual devotion. To the point that they were not happy when I appeared in the picture because of the threat I posed to everything. Outsiders... we don't always understand. It got out of hand. My mother-in-law, she was not well and borderline evil. But I have grasped what they mean to the Z."

"Dr. Chen." Someone must have corrected Kelton about my title since the last time I'd spoken to him. "We all owe you an apology."

I shook my head. "Don't owe me an apology. Believe me now. They're not dead. I'm not deluded. I'm not in shock. They are still alive. Somehow. Somewhere."

"Amber," Paloma spoke slowly. I fully expected her to argue. "I believe you and not because you asked me to. When they told me Tommy and Quinn were dead I could feel inside they weren't. I knew they lived. I couldn't accept otherwise. I believe you. Maybe it's something we can do. In our family. Maybe we can somehow feel it. Deep inside of us."

Melissa sighed. "We're getting reports that there are captives. I don't know how many or if it's possible..."

There was the answer. "It is. Trust me. They'd have fought it, but if there was a way the Z on that ship could have arranged for my husbands to be saved, they'd have done it."

Kelton crossed his arms over his chest. "Absolutely true. I believe you. Can you speak to them, Amber? Does it go that far?"

"I wish it did. No, it's more like I can just feel them."

"How do we find them? We know they're alive." Diana looked between us. "Do we just go to the Dark Planets and start looking? I'm up for that. But is there a more... strategic way we could go about this?"

They believed me. No one here had argued, no one acted like I didn't know what I was talking about. I let out a breath I'd held. Okay. We'd get through this.

Waverly looked around. "What do they still want? They haven't gone through the hole. There must be someone they still want here, a reason they went to the Dark Planets. I don't believe it's just to regroup and try again. I mean, we must have cost them a huge amount in resources."

Melissa rubbed her face. "I honestly don't have the slightest idea what Peter Aron wants. He's the current CEO. The person in charge keeps changing. We had the info on the last one and then that stopped being meaningful."

My ears buzzed. "We do know. We don't know why but we know what... sorry, who. We know who. They want Sienna MacKinnon. In fact, I bet they have my husbands because they think they know where she is. They really don't." Goosebumps broke out on my arms. "And we never wanted them to."

That was what Ari had meant. Don't tell them. Don't let them know when I took her, don't wake her, don't let my husbands really know or understand anything about her. I put my hands on my knees. I had to breathe. Of course future Ari knew something would happen. The question was why. Was it important they not know because that would keep them alive or because some kind of future plan required them to die?

Well, fuck that second choice, and I didn't believe that Ari would do that to me. He wouldn't set me up to have them killed. That was ridiculous. I had to go with the latter. The best possible reasons for why this happened.

I hated time travel.

Paloma rubbed my back. "Maybe you should take a break."

"No." I stood fast. "I'm fine."

Thomas stepped through the doorway, catching all of our attention. I hadn't heard him come but I wasn't surprised he would. Not if Paloma was here and shaken, as she must have been by what happened to me. "So they're looking for Artemis. Let's assume for a second that they know the ship and Sienna on it are in the Dark Planets, they head out there. That doesn't help us. Blaze is in charge of that ship. He has Trenton. Two other Super Soldiers and Wade, who is quiet but motivated. We can't find Artemis by just running out into the Dark Planets and looking. We'll never find him. Blaze, as he demonstrated again and again over the last months, is a strategic genius. He isn't going to let himself be found."

Melissa whirled around. "We can find Artemis. We absolutely can. I... I can't believe it, but I one hundred percent can find Artemis even if Blaze jumps the ship around the Dark Planets every ten minutes."

"I told you it would come in handy," C.J. spoke from the shadows. The spymaster would never miss this. I really wasn't meant to lead if I couldn't see these things clearly. "I told you, M, that it wouldn't be a waste of time and money. Finding and taking the ship called *Malice* with us was good luck."

She smiled at him. "I should know not to doubt your instincts after all of these years."

Damian stepped out of the shadows on the other side, standing next to Diana. "Forgive me, but how does having Malice make a difference? I mean, Blaze isn't going to suddenly see the ship and decide to come out of hiding."

"Malice can find Artemis," C.J. explained. "Listen, the history of these ships is really interesting. They weren't highly thought of designs so they only made five. I couldn't believe it when I saw Malice. What is she doing on this side of the galaxy? How did she get over here?"

"With me, actually." Jackson walked in. We had really brought a crowd. "Malice is the ship I stowed away on to get across the galaxy a million years ago. A bunch of pirates were in control of it then. They didn't kill me, taught me a bunch of things on how to build, engineer, pilot. Then dropped me off on a cold wasteland of a planet on the edge of the Dark Planets to make my way or not. Is she here?"

C.J. grinned. "Well, that explains that. Anyway, Malice and Artemis, the designer, a man named Danny Rutter, was years ahead of his time. I met him twice."

Melissa cleared her throat. "C.J."

"Right, sorry. Okay. So, the ships can always locate each other. He thought he was doing us all a favor, knowing it would be the rebels who took the ships, and we'd like to find each other. We didn't much care for that, actually. We mostly were out for just ourselves. That quirk in the ships turned out to be why they weren't sought after that. Melissa took Artemis, but the others went out to people who wouldn't give a shit. Pirates, apparently. I can't say as I've ever met a pirate."

Jackson held up his hand. "Nice to meet you."

"Malice can find Artemis. Great. We find Artemis and convince Blaze to help us by bringing Artemis out in the open to draw out Evander and from there find my guys."

Melissa nodded. "It's a pretty solid plan. Let's get this started."

Kelton nodded to her. "We will do this. They are our leaders, our friends, our family. We will go get them. Thank you for this. Please stay here and heal from the ordeal you've been through."

Melissa shook her head. "Amari saved our lives, twice. If he's out there being held prisoner, then my job isn't done. We'll be going to help you."

Kelton bent his head slightly. "Thank you."

"You're welcome."

I held up my hand. "I'm going, too."

All eyes were suddenly on me. "Well, I'm not staying here and waiting any longer. You'll need a doctor. Woody is dead. I'm going."

"Amber." Melissa took my hand. "Are you sure?"

"Am I sure? Yes, I'm sure. I've made these babies as safe as I can make them. I have the implant, thanks to Hunter, Lewis, Ari and Diana. It's doing its job. I am going to come and help." I pointed my index finger at Melissa. "And don't you for one second tell me I can't. I know all about the things you were doing when you were pregnant with Diana. We've all heard the stories. Nine months pregnant running around, taking on your mother, piloting Artemis all by yourself, shoving your husbands through the black hole. You can't tell me that pregnant women can't do as they like. The babies are safe right now. I'm going. Period."

Melissa held up both her hands. "I really wish you all hadn't heard those stories. Yes, you're right. You can do whatever you think you can do, and you can keep those girls safe in the meantime. We'll get your husbands back."

———

I stood next to Ari, studying Malice. Behind me, Chrissy cried softly as she said goodbye to Brenden. They were going to get married when we returned. That was super sweet, but my small headache and the fact that Brenden had never left during the whole war somewhat negated my sympathy for her. Or maybe I was just in a really bad mood.

"Canyon wants to talk to you," Ari informed me.

I turned to regard him. "Oh. Where is he?"

"Waiting to make sure it's okay."

I didn't understand. "Why wouldn't it be okay?"

"Because you might be angry with me." Canyon walked over. "I screwed with your life."

He had? "I'm not sure I know what you mean."

Ari nodded, stepping away. Canyon was very intense, all the Super Soldiers were. Still, we'd all come to be friends on The Farm. Whatever he needed to get out, he should say. I hated the idea that he thought he couldn't talk to me. His wife was one of my closest friends. She stood in the corner, leaning against Ari as they both pretended not to watch.

"Canyon? Whatever it is just get to it."

"I got caught in their tablet on purpose. When you asked me to get the letters, I could have done that easily without being noticed. In fact, I had. I had the letters. And then I read them because, as Waverly reminded me when I fessed up recently, I don't always understand boundaries.

You'd asked me to help you with a private thing. I shouldn't have read anything. Anyway, I did. And I thought that whoever wrote you those letters had to love you the way I love the light in my life. It was obvious. So I went back in and got caught, suspecting that I'd draw their attention and you could all work that out."

Well, that answered a question I hadn't even known I still had at this point. "I see."

"And it seemed like they did. At first I thought I'd made a terrible mistake with the abuse allegations, but then you said they hadn't been the ones to hurt you, and Hunter killed the fucking man who did. I really liked them during the war. I didn't make a mistake, right? You are happy to have had them back, it worked?"

I put my hand on his arm, and I squeezed. "Thank you. I would have had such a colorless life without them. I had all this love for them and nowhere to put it, nowhere to give it. I thought it wasn't returned. It was. I... Thank you, Canyon. For not respecting my boundaries. I wouldn't make a habit out of it. I mean, other situations might not turn out the same. But I thank you."

He nodded. "I'm so relieved. Still, there is something I'd like to do for you. I'd like to help."

"No." I'd been adamant with my sister, Waverly, and Diana. They'd just gotten their families back. We didn't know where Evander was and we might need them to fight in the Dark Planets in a not too distant time. They needed time together. "You're staying here."

He sighed. "I know. And I appreciate that you want that for us. I do. So what I propose is helping you, but not *now*."

"Is this a time travel thing?"

He gave me a wide smile. "It is. We will, sometime in

the future, travel back to the moment you are rescuing your husbands, and we will in some way help. This won't be interfering with the past, per se, because we will have done it already so when we go to do it, we will have already done it. Make sense?"

"No." I rubbed the back of my neck. "I hate time travel. It makes my head hurt."

"Everyone says that. I love it." He shrugged. "Count on our help. We've already messed with your life. Ari giving cryptic messages on Artemis is very odd for us. So we have to assume you're very important. Well, we already know that. You kept this place afloat. We won the battle for Earth and that is not in any small part thanks to you."

I'd officially gotten uncomfortable. That strange, unsettled, I didn't know how to react feeling settled in my stomach. I didn't do compliments well. "Thank you. And if you can help... now or in the future... without risking yourselves so that Waverly loses everything... then I thank you for that, too."

He nodded. "Good luck, Amber Chen. I believe you will bring them home."

I hoped he was right.

———

I didn't tell anyone on the ship about Canyon's help. The Z didn't know about the time travel and as much as I now officially believed in the Zansi, that wasn't my secret to tell. I could have told Melissa but she was holed up in the back of the ship with her husbands and her oldest son, Asher, who joined on this trip. He was officially an adult now and wasn't going to be left behind. He'd saved me years before on my run across the galaxy to escape from Earth. He'd apparently fought bravely in the war.

And still I had trouble thinking of him as a grown up.

They were all quietly busy. Melissa had left her other children to do this, apparently deciding to put them in school on the Venus colony where I'd been born, and where Wade's brother and sister studied. It was safe there, and unless Evander came traipsing over again, they should stay that way. I'd looked away when she'd teared up after dropping them there. There were some moments that were private.

I played cards with Brenden, Matt, Kenton, and the others. The members of the Z who were not my guards seemed like they were trying to bond with me. Maybe the idea that I might be utterly in charge of them for eighteen years was enough to make them begin.

Amari left Kelton in charge of the business when he left. He was smart and kept winning at cards. I didn't really know the game. I did, however, notice how Kelton and Matt looked at each other. They were definitely together. Like the rest of us, they'd been separated during the battle. My insistence on coming along had let them be together, too.

Of course neither of them had told me they were together. I was speculating. But I was right. I was sure of it.

"Amber," Kelton spoke my name. "Is it okay if I use your first name? I've heard both Brenden and Matt do it accidently. You don't object. Is it okay?"

I cleared my throat. "I don't mind. Everyone can call me Amber. My husbands won't like it, though. They seem to care a great deal about the protocol with me. Maybe because of everything that happened?"

Kelton nodded. "Well, I won't do it if they don't like it.

For now, I'll call you Amber. The Masters Chen can tell me to stop. Amber, I was thinking..."

"A dangerous pastime for him." Matt winked at me, and Kelton laughed. This was officially the most relaxed I'd ever seen the Z.

Kelton threw down his cards. "As I was saying before I was rudely interrupted by brown eyes over there, it isn't a huge step to go from what you are describing, feeling them, to talking to them. Not through the energy barrier."

"The energy barrier?"

Brenden shook his head. "It's a term we learned in training and school. It doesn't really matter. You're doing the act anyway, and I can barely do it at all. It's more of a Chen thing."

"He can do it, a little." Matt grinned, pointing at Kelton.

"I have the smallest amount of Chen blood. We're third cousins. Yes, but not like you're doing it. Tell me, could you do it before you were pregnant?" Kelton took a drink of his coffee.

That stopped me short. "I could see they vibrated. Hunter thought I'd have a natural affinity for it. But no, I couldn't feel them."

"Well, maybe you have some Chen blood running through you right now. Two of them. For the next eight months."

I leaned forward. "Are you suggesting that my unborn daughters who are currently the size of cherries are why I can do this meditation thing where I feel them?"

He shrugged. "Maybe. You should see if you can push through to the actual talking. Maybe they could help us know where they are."

Brenden looked between us. "It's a huge step."

"She communicated energy in next to no time. I don't think it's impossible she could do this."

Well, I could certainly try. And Kelton and Matt were totally together. I'd been right about that.

———

I sat on the floor of my room. Malice wasn't as nice a ship as Artemis. It had clearly never had much of a woman's touch on it. The registrar that C.J. pulled out said that it had actually had a Sandler owner at some point. I was going to have to ask Paloma who that was someday.

I put my hand on my stomach. "Are you ladies making this happen by just existing?" I took a deep breath. "Okay, let's see if we can do this. Push through? How am I supposed to do that?"

I closed my eyes, concentrating on my breathing. My hands tingled. My pulse steadied. I actually had grown to like this part. Hunter had been right. It was calming. Eventually, I reached the point where I had to try.

I sent my energy out to them with my love. It took a second but it was like Amari was all over me. I loved that feeling. Hunter was next and then Shane right after. Oh thank the universe, they were all still okay.

I tried again. There was an energy barrier? The words made me disgruntled. I didn't know what that meant. I didn't care. I liked how this felt. I wanted more. I wanted to link my energy to theirs. I pushed a little bit harder.

I spoke. "Can you guys hear me?"

Amber... It sounded like Hunter. But then it was over.

I sighed. I guessed I'd done it. I'd heard my name in my head with Hunter's voice. That was amazing. There was no doubt in my mind my husband could do this. That just meant the weak link was me.

I leaned back on the floor. I could do this. I just had to keep working. My yawn surprised me. I'd been doing a pretty good job of keeping my pregnancy symptoms at bay. I had yet to throw up, even though I'd had moments where I thought I might. And I'd pushed through the exhaustion.

Now, however, I couldn't even seem to muster the energy to get off the floor.

I closed my eyes and went to sleep right there on the floor.

I dreamed of a blonde woman running through a space-ship. "Amber, I think it's time to wake me up now. I don't see how it can be put off anymore."

I smiled at her. "Sienna, you're not my patient any longer. Wade will know what to do."

"Thank you, Amber." She hugged me tightly. "Thank you for keeping me safe as long as you did."

I TOUCHED the walls of Malice. This ship probably had stories like Artemis did. Had she made families the way that her sister ship had? Kelton told me they'd picked up Artemis' signal and were following it. He thought we'd be there in two days, assuming Blaze didn't travel too far.

There was no sign of Evander, but given that their last ship had appeared out of nowhere, we were being very careful. A ship like ours wasn't likely to draw their attention. We'd be junk to them, not a resource.

Hopefully we'd remain ignored. After eating, I headed back to my room to try to meditate again. That seemed to be the best use of my time, which was strange but at least it gave me something to do.

I breathed. I'd have to check and see if all this breathing was doing anything for me in other ways. I didn't have a blood pressure problem, but maybe it was even better. I'd figure that out later. I breathed. It certainly had to be good for the babies that I was spending so much time in a relaxed matter.

Or pretending to relax. That had to count for something.

When I felt the moment come, a total awareness of my body, I sent my love out to the guys. This time I could feel it when it hit them, like a zap through my whole system.

"Can you feel her?" Hunter moaned, his voice sounded hoarse. "I can feel her."

"Yes," Amari and Hunter answered together.

The rush of their love filled me, and I could have cried for the joy of it. Hearing their voices was such a gift.

"Guys." I really wanted them to be able to hear me, too. "Can you hear me? I can hear you."

I was pretty sure Hunter took in an audible breath. "Amber? Can... can you hear us?"

I wiped away my tears. "I can. I've been working on this."

"This is incredible. Guys, can you hear her?"

"I can," Amari said. "Shane's out cold. He can't hear anything right now."

I sucked in my breath. "Why is Shane out cold?"

"Don't worry, love." Hunter caught my attention. "He'll be fine. He's just sleeping."

I didn't believe him. For almost never lying, when they did they were really, really bad at it. But I didn't want this to be stressful, and I had a feeling I was going to have to lie to them, too. I swallowed. "Are you guys okay?"

"We're fine. Don't worry about us," Amari answered this time. "How did you learn how to do this?"

That I could answer. "I meditated. Kelton thinks it's the girls. He thinks the fact that they're in my uterus has given me enough Chen blood to do this."

They were so silent for a minute I thought maybe they were gone, but Hunter finally spoke. "That's just amazing."

"It is. Listen, my loves, because I could feel you I was able to tell everyone you weren't dead, and thank the universe they believed me. I guess this has to do with energy barriers." I hoped I was sounding upbeat enough. "They're coming for you." I left myself out of it. There was the lie. If they didn't want me to worry, I didn't want them too, either. "Is there anything you can tell me that might help them locate you faster?"

Amari cleared his throat. "We're in constant motion. They're bouncing around wherever they are. And... I don't know if they should attempt this, love. It was the most over-whelming battle imaginable. If any of them got out of there, then I am relieved. Tell them I want them to rebuild. I want them to protect you and the girls. I want them to rebuild the Earth and protect the water. Tell them we're too far gone to be saved. I'm sorry. That isn't what I want to be saying to you. If there's any chance, we'll still try to escape. I'm afraid that by the time they can find us, it'll be too late. I don't want them doing that when they should be guarding you."

I cried, I didn't even try to wipe away the tears. "I don't think they're going to accept that, and I'm not telling them that, no. Sorry, Master Chen. I don't take orders from you. They tell me I'm in charge now."

"Fuck, listen to me, Amber."

I shook my head. "No, you listen to me, you two, and Shane if he can hear me. I love you more than anything. The girls will love you that way, too. You're coming home. You promised me. All three of you did. So you hold on. They have a plan to find you. And if you can't help, then you don't help. You just stay as you are and hold on."

"Amber," Amari's voice broke which almost destroyed me. "I fucking love you. I'm sorry. I'm always failing. I did promise we'd come home. We'll hold on as long as we can. I promise you that. There's nothing I want more than to just be home with you."

I sucked in my tears and tried to send just love instead. "Your cousin cheats at cards. I'm convinced."

Hunter laughed. "He does."

This was better. This was what they needed to hold onto. "You should have seen the Sandlers coming back. It was such a scene. They had a huge fight because they couldn't find Paloma. I had to manage that. Then everyone got drunk. Well, not me. I'm obviously not drinking. And Hunter, your design worked. The babies are safe inside of me with the machine constantly fixing it from the inside out."

"Inside of you?" Hunter's voice lightened. "Really? I didn't even think of that. Who converted my design? I need to thank him."

"Ari and Lewis. Guys, the water is fine." Or it was before I left.

"Shit," Amari's voice was low. "The ticking is louder, saying the elevator is coming. Amber, we need to cut this off. I don't want them to know we can do this. I love you."

Hunter sighed. "I hate the ticking on this ship. Yes, love you. And Shane loves you, too."

My energy flew back into me. Dizziness wafted through me, and I thought I might faint. I pulled my knees to my forehead. Okay. I had information to give over to Kelton and Melissa. I'd lied to them, and I didn't feel bad about it. Something was wrong with Shane. He'd been awake, and he'd passed out. He would never have done that, never not spoken to me if he could have stayed awake. We were all covering up what would be the most concerning.

Nothing would break Amari short of something happening to his brothers. Or me. I pulled myself up and sat on my bed. I wasn't making it to the door. This energy thing took a lot out of me. I grabbed my wrist, poking the chip that would let me communicate with others on Malice.

"Brenden, I need help."

The door opened instantly. I should have known he'd been outside the whole time. Nothing had changed just because we were on the ship. He was letting me think I got to wander by myself but he was there.

"Amber?" He walked straight to me. "What's wrong?"

"I talked to them and now I'm dizzy. Hand me my scanner. It's over next to the bed."

The head of my Z did as I asked. I quickly scanned myself. Dane was here. He'd help if I needed it. All of the numbers were good. The babies were good. This was just overwhelming exhaustion from whatever had taken place.

"I'm going to nap." I handed him the scanner. "I don't have a choice. Between the pregnancy and this, I'm done. Listen, tell Kelton and Melissa the Chens are being tortured. They didn't say it, but I can tell. Shane is injured. They're in constant movement. That's all I could tell."

Brenden nodded. "Right away. Rest. I don't want them to kill me when we get them back."

I crawled to the center of the bed, face planting into my pillow.

———

A hand touched my shoulder, and I darted awake. Melissa sat down on the edge of my bed. "I'm sorry. I remember the exhaustion you're under. I did it once with twins, too." She stroked my hair. "I keep thinking we should get in touch with your mother, but if you'd wanted that you'd have done it."

It was nice to have her here. I was sure she hadn't come in to offer me comfort, but I'd take it for a minute if she was doling out babying.

"I don't want to talk to her. I know Paloma made some kind of peace with her, but I don't want to see her. Maybe ever again. I'm sorry if that makes me... hard."

She shook her head. "I am the last person to tell anyone how to treat their parents. You have plenty of reasons to want to be done. Well, we've found Artemis, and we are going to try to get Blaze's attention. I thought you might want to be here for this."

I sat up. "I do. Thanks. This is Blaze. So let me ask you, do you think there's any chance Blaze—the Super Soldier and master strategist—is not fully aware that our ship is here?"

She grinned. "Oh, he knows. We just need him to talk to us. That is frequently the hardest part. If he ignores us and won't take our messages, we might have to fire."

They were going to fire on Blaze? Yes, I had to get up. Not that I could do anything, but I didn't want to be lying in my room asleep if we suddenly got into a battle with a Super Soldier, all of us in old ships that had once been created together.

━━

"Who wants to talk?" C.J. spun around in his chair. "Who knows Blaze best? Is it you, M?"

"I know him but not best. He dealt much more with Amari than me, which was fine by me because other than my son-in-law, I find the Super Soldiers to be really scary, if I'm being honest."

I waved my hand at her in dismissal. "Look at Rohan

and Canyon. They're all just looking for love like the rest of us, to feel human, to feel... wanted, purposeful. Normal."

She laughed. "That may be true, but I'm here to tell you the time it takes to get them to the point where they can even speak to women is scary. The three on that ship are not there yet."

"Does it have to be Blaze? I know Wade pretty well."

C.J. pointed at the control. "Go say hi. See if they answer."

I touched the talk button. It was important to do new things all the time. Someone had told me that. This was the very first time I'd hit a button and spoke into the vastness of space to hope a hidden ship answered.

It was more than slightly intimidating.

"Hi, Artemis, this is Amber Chen. Hi. I hope you can hear me. We're here to talk. I know you have reason to be suspicious, but I think almost all of you know me and..."

Malice's screen turned on. Blaze stood there, his arms crossed over his chest. "Stop. Secure channel now."

Melissa answered him. "We don't know your channels. We've been trying."

"Where is Amari? He knows them." He hit some numbers and a secure channel appeared on Melissa's tablet. I didn't want to know how he knew how to do that. She entered the channel and the conversation continued.

"That's why we're here. They have my husbands."

His face fell. "Come aboard."

The screen faded. I looked at Melissa. "I guess we're going aboard."

"It would seem that way."

There had been something in Blaze's expression when I said Amari was missing. He'd cared. Those Super Soldiers might not be so far from ready to join society as she thought.

At the end of the day, what mattered was how we cared about each other.

———

I didn't know why I was able to take a deep breath when we boarded Artemis. Malice had been a great ship, done just what we needed, but somehow Artemis just felt better to me. Maybe because in her walls I'd found my husbands again—well, really for the first time. It was as though nothing bad could happen there.

In the conference room, Melissa faltered and laughed. "Someone painted?"

"Kellan can't stand disorder. The walls peeling... bothered him." Blaze nodded toward the other Super Soldier. "He fixed it. So Amari is missing."

We'd been wrong when we thought there were three Super Soldiers on the ship. There were four. Blaze. Anders. Kellan. Corbin. All four of them. They were often together, although Blaze was always in charge. Trenton joined us in the room, and I spoke. I still hadn't seen Wade.

"It's not just Amari. Shane. Hunter, too. I've communicated with them." I wasn't going to elaborate. Next to me, Kelton nodded slightly. He agreed. We were keeping my abilities to myself. For now, anyway. "We are looking to draw Evander out."

"Oh, I see." Anders looked between us. "You want us to expose ourselves to Evander."

I nodded. "We do."

"Evander wants this woman. They want her so much they are chasing us through the galaxy. There is every chance they are out there right now. They appear out of nowhere. They have some sort of... cloak. I like your husbands very much. However, I care a great deal more that Evander not get whoever it is they want. They aren't interested in her just because she's beautiful. Or because she'd bring a lot of money on a marriage mart. Any female would do that on the other side of the galaxy; there are so few left." He shook his head. "There is something about Sienna. The more any of us spend time around her unconscious form, the more we are certain of it. Wade has been the most affected."

I cleared my throat. "Affected how?"

"When we're done here, you should go see him. Judge for yourself. He's functioning fine. A very good doctor, but it's obvious that the more time in her presence he gets, the more his situation increases. I have no answer for it."

I was interested in this but not until we settled this with Blaze. "What if we changed ships? You took Sienna and went onto Malice. We stayed here. Exposed ourselves to Evander. She's not at risk and you have more of an edge because now they don't know what ship you're on."

Corbin looked at Blaze. "That's not a bad idea."

Trenton cleared his throat. "There's a hit out, so to speak, on Artemis. There isn't one on Malice. I could take Malice to any space station and hide us. Or planet. I like Amber's plan."

I'd never met Trenton before recently, but he was Ari's friend. I could see why. They both looked like they'd been through hell and come out the other side beaten up but still standing. What was his story? Not like I had time to ask. Maybe later.

"Then that is what we do." Blaze nodded. "We'll switch..."

An alarm sounded and everyone spun around. Trenton held up a tablet. "Evander is here."

Blaze nodded. "It's the big ship. They have some system that allows them to fog up space. It was awful. But we got away."

"We're familiar with it," Melissa spoke through clenched teeth.

"Not again," C.J. jumped up. "Cooper."

Melissa's quietest husband rushed to the tablet. We were on Artemis. What was he going to do? "I can control Malice from here. Helps that we're all not on that ship."

I was enormously grateful to have left my cat at home. Blaze hit a button and Cooper's tablet displayed on the screen in front of us. Malice spun in a circle before it pushed out a black smoke I'd never seen before.

'What's happening?"

"This is what Hunter did," Cooper supplied without looking up. "This is how you battle it."

Anders tilted his head. "Fascinating."

Next to the main ship, five small ships appeared. They were old, sort of decrepit looking. "What are those?"

Melissa scowled. "They keep their cleanup crews on those. They don't care if they live or die. They won't fire, and we leave them alone. If we disable the main ship they just kind of float dead in the air. Huge problem when planning during battles. It was Amari who figured out to leave them alone. Waste of resources to bother with them."

It sounded like Amari had figured out how to think like Evander did. That didn't surprise me in the least.

"We go on that ship." Kelton turned around. "They'll know where the Chens are. We're disabling it. Come on. We go on."

"Good thought." Blaze grabbed a weapon and strapped it to his waist. "Let's do this."

I didn't have a thing to say. Everyone was leaving the

ship except Brenden and Matt. My head Z shook his head at me. "Don't. Too much of a risk for you. Stop and think about it. Just because you can doesn't mean you should."

He was right. "Okay. I'll stay here and see what is going on with Wade."

Anxiety fueled my steps. We might have been getting the answers we needed right now. Or the part of me that was hopeful somehow wondered if they were on that ship. Probably not. But maybe.

Wade stared out the window at the ship we were getting ready to board. He turned to look at me. "Amber. I'm so glad to see you."

He had dark circles under his eyes. I wanted to scan him immediately. What happened here?

"Are you okay?"

Wade shook his head. "I don't know, actually."

"Blaze indicated that something might be very wrong. He thought it might be because of Sienna. Talk to me. I need the distraction. Let me check you out."

Wade pointed at the med machine. "Sienna is in there. I took her out of cryogenic sleep but the machine is keeping her under because she has the flu. GH231-01 flu."

I shuddered. The Gs were all fatal. We couldn't cure them, not one, not ever. I walked over to look down at her. "Do you think you've somehow caught the flu?"

"No. I feel fine."

I put my hand on his forehead. He didn't feel warm. "Something is wrong with you, Wade. That's my medical opinion without having run a scan."

"I can't sleep, Amber."

That was fixable. I put my hands on my hips. "Shall I prescribe you something?"

"No." He walked over and looked down at Sienna. "I'm sure I could sleep if I let myself."

This was getting more and more bizarre. It had absolutely taken my mind off the fact that everyone had invaded an Evander ship.

Amber...

A female voice swept through my mind, and I jumped. That wasn't my voice, and it wasn't my husbands. What in the hell was that?

I spun around and Wade pointed at me. "You heard her."

Okay. My heart was in my throat. "I heard something."

He shook his head fast. "You heard it. I know you did."

I pointed at the unconscious woman. "Was that Sienna? How was that Sienna?"

"I don't know. She talks to me. In my head." He pointed to his forehead. "The others can't hear her. They don't. They've all gotten very protective of her. But I was the only lunatic hearing voices until you just did. You did."

I nodded. "I did. I heard her voice."

He sagged. "I thought I was going to have to go away somewhere, but I don't want to leave her. Why don't I want to leave her? She's a patient. I've had thousands of patients. I've been a doctor since I was twenty. I treated patients while Evander locked me away. I don't get attached. Maybe I don't have a heart."

He grabbed his head. "She says I have a heart."

"Maybe we need to step away." I took his hand. "She's okay. We're going to leave her for a minute or two. We're going to go out in the hall."

The ships outside turned, and as they did, I twisted to look at them through the window in the hall. Wade covered his eyes with his hands. "There have never been any reputable examples of psychic ability recorded in human history. It doesn't exist."

"It does, Wade." I had an example of it in my own life. "I've seen it, and I'm not easily swayed. I won't get into the details."

He leaned against the wall. "This is why they want her. I bet she's recordable. They want her to be some kind of weapon. I could ask her, but I don't dare. I won't really talk to her. I don't answer. She talks, hears me if I say things, but I don't talk to her. That's too far. I won't. She can talk in my head, and she's dying. Is it because of the flu?"

"Wade... I..."

My tablet dinged, and I turned it on for a message from Melissa. "We're in a battle we're winning. So far no signs of the Chens."

A loud ticking noise assaulted my ears. "What is that sound?"

"The cleaning ships. They're attached via speaker. It's obnoxious. A terrible sound. Hold steady, Amber. If there's something to find we'll find it."

She disconnected. A ticking noise. Tic. Tic. Tic. Fuck, that was what my husbands had said. I tried Melissa back, but I got nothing. They were in a battle.

"What happens to the ships, the cleaning ships, if the big one fails?" I stormed toward the docking bay without even thinking.

"Where are you going?" Wade called after me.

I didn't answer him, grabbing onto Brenden's arm when he caught up with me. "They're on one of those ships. The ticking. They told me about the ticking. They're on there. We have to go find them. I'm worried about it. They're... I can't explain it. Intuition. Maybe I'm fucking psychic. We have to go."

Brenden touched his ear. "I can't get anyone on the line. Are you sure?"

"How can I be sure? I'll never be sure. But somehow I know. Brenden, we have to go."

He held up his hands. "Come on. You and me. I'll keep calling the others. We'll get through. They'll meet us there. This is insanity. They're going to kill me." He wasn't talking to me anymore. "I'm supposed to guard you but I never can. You throw yourself into danger. You never stop. And I respect every decision you make."

Matt ran up next to us. "Where are we going?"

"The cleanup ships. Get your fiancé on the line. I can't reach him."

I swung around. "This is not important right now, but I knew it."

Matt touched his ear. "Too much interference. We're going to the broken down ships."

We were. If I was wrong, I'd never insist anyone had to do anything again. I'd sit still and keep quiet, letting the experts run this. My body buzzed. They were close to me. My energy called out to theirs. I sent them love. I wasn't meditating, but it felt like I could.

The smallest love came back. One of them. Hunter. The others had faded. This was bad. "Hurry, Brenden. Get us there fast."

"I will." He nodded.

"I can feel them, sort of. They're not okay." I paced back and forth. I couldn't make anything go any faster. I grabbed onto my knees.

Hold on guys. Just hold on a little bit longer.

"I DON'T KNOW how we're going to get on," Brenden muttered as we pulled up alongside the ship. "It's not like they're going to simply open the doors for us. We're going to have to blow a hole and we don't know where..."

His voice trailed off. I stepped up next to him. "What?"

"The cargo bay door just opened."

Matt scrunched up his face. "Is that a good thing or a bad thing?"

The lights on the ship turned off and on twice. If we'd been back on The Farm that would have been the signal for all clear. Canyon had said they would help us. My breathing picked up. "It's safe. Trust me. I know I'm asking a lot, but a friend opened those doors. Sometime in the distant future, I'll maybe explain it to you."

Brenden shot me a look that told me he didn't like that answer, but he docked our shuttle just the same. A moment of anxiety passed through me that I pushed away. We boarded the cleaning ship and as I stepped off, I spotted him.

It *was* Canyon. He nodded to me before he vanished.

When I got back, I was going to thank him over and over again. Of course, he hadn't done this yet. He would do it. But just the same.

They didn't interfere too strongly in the past for fear of Evander discovering the technology. This, they'd been able to do.

That also meant I was right. My guys were here.

Brenden and Matt pulled out their laser-targeted guns. I'd never actually seen the Z use weapons before, but I supposed it made sense. We weren't in a hand-to-hand combat situation and maybe they weren't as fast as the others in moving energy.

Matt touched his ear. "The communications are back up. Master Kelton, can you hear me?" That was his fiancé but in this situation they were back to holding rank. "I'm on the service ship with Dr. Chen and Brenden. The Chens are here." He winced and looked at me. "He's not happy." He spoke to Kelton again. "You're in the middle of a battle, and we couldn't reach you. We're fine so far. No resistance."

I smiled. That might have been Canyon, too. Small touches of things that could go unnoticed, but made a huge difference. The ship made the loudest ticking noise I'd ever heard. I bit down on my lip. How had they tolerated this for so long?

Weeks like this would have driven me mad. I closed my eyes. Where were they? I could only feel Hunter, and I wasn't going to dwell too long on why that was. Amari and Shane were okay. They were just... hurt. They needed me.

I pointed at the elevator. "They're below."

Brenden nodded. "Come on."

Like my guys had said, the ticking got noisier when the elevator was in use. Matt winced. "We need to get them out of here and fast. This place is not steady. I don't want

Kelton to come chasing me after I'm dead to kill me for getting you killed."

I shook my head. "He would be upset at me, that is for sure, but more upset to lose you."

Matt looked down at his feet. "We're all loyal to the Z and the Chens first and foremost."

I touched his arm. "I know you are. But it's perfectly fine to put love in there, too. I would never expect you to pick me over the love of your life. And don't argue. I'm risking all of you to go get my three."

The elevator stopped at the bottom floor. Fortunately, this ship was small enough that we didn't have to try to determine which floor to go to. The first thing as we stepped off the elevator was the smell. I gagged and then covered my mouth. The people being held here were not being cared for. Death, disease, feces, vomit. It overwhelmed me for a second, but I pulled it together. My sense of smell was heightened, thanks to the girls, and it took me a moment to adjust. People moaned in the distance.

I nodded. "I have to be. Come on. Matt, can you get us some help? Anyone leave the other ship? There are a lot of people here."

He touched his ear. "Master Kelton, we need assistance. Dr. Chen is fine but there are lot of captives."

He spoke for a while, but I didn't listen, heading instead to the cages that held Evander's captives all over the room. Most people were unconscious, which was a small kindness for them. Behind me, Brenden jiggled keys.

"I found them by the elevator."

I touched his arm. "Start opening these up. When Kelton gets here with help, we can all start loading these poor people onto the shuttles. We're going to need the med bays on both Artemis and Malice. Call over to Wade. Let him know to get ready and tell Dane that if he can steal any med machines from Evander on the other ship that will likely be helpful."

He nodded. "On it."

I kept walking forward. Evander didn't have to keep guards, not when the prisoners were so sick and dying. I kept my anticipation down. I had to stay present and not rush through here like a lunatic looking for them.

"Mrs. Chen," a small voice caught my attention and I looked down at a Z Warrior whose name I didn't know.

I squatted in front of him. "We're here to help you. Brenden is coming. He'll let you out and medical assistance is on the way."

"They're two down from here. I tried to save them. I got them on the shuttle. I had to hit Master Shane, but that's my job. The Z always have some of us assigned." He started to choke uncontrollably.

I put my hand through the bars and held onto his. "Thank you. What's your name?"

Brenden was right next to me. "This is Bill. He's been with us a long time."

"You took care of her," Bill managed to squeak.

"Get him out." I rose and passed the next cage where the man in it was unconscious. But seeing my three stopped me short. Shane was in the first cage. He didn't move or look up when I passed him. Amari was in the middle, his arm slung down hitting the floor. Hunter was awake, and as I came into view of him in the last cage, he tried and failed, to sit up.

"Don't move," I commanded him. "Not an inch."

"How?"

Brenden opened the cages, and I scooted inside to Hunter. I needed to check on the other two, but Hunter was awake, and if I needed information, I was going to get it from him.

The ticking increased, and I hoped that meant Kelton and his crew were coming down the elevator.

Hunter smiled at me; his eyes weren't clear. "I had a feeling you were lying. You were on your way here."

I nodded. "And you lied when you said they were okay."

"I don't know if they are. I can't tell if Shane is breathing anymore."

His words broke my heart. "They both still are, and the good news, my love, is that you married a doctor. I'm going to take good care of all of you. Help is here."

He winced. "I don't know that I have much energy left to hold on. But I am so glad I got to see your face one more time."

"Oh no. Don't talk like this. I get it. You have to be exhausted but you made me a promise you'd come home, and you are keeping it. End of story. What happened to you guys?"

His breathing was shallow. I wanted him in the med machine yesterday and my other two husbands with him immediately. Still, I kept my face calm. "They injected us with something. Feels like my insides are burning. That's when Amari lost it." He winced. "He doesn't pass out. Ever."

I wiped away the sweat on his forehead. This was Evander torture. They injected all kinds of diseases into people. I had no idea what it was yet, but suddenly Kelton was there.

"Dr. Chen. We'll grab them. All of them." I bent over to kiss Hunter on the cheek. "I'm going to see you really soon even though you won't remember it because we're going to knock you into sweet dreams. When you wake up, it'll be over, and you'll be home." I kissed his other cheek. "I love you."

Hunter tried to speak, but his eyes rolled to the back of his head. I somehow managed not to scream.

I passed him to Kelton, who picked him up to carry him. Shane and Amari were already en route to the elevator, Shane in Matt's arms, and Amari in Brenden's. I wanted to rush after them, to get to the med bay to get started in healing them, but I had to be smart about this.

I didn't have a clue what they could have been injected into them that made them burn. I grabbed my ear piece. "Dane, can you hear me? Wade?"

Both of them answered at once. Wade with a *yes* and Dane with a *talk to me*. Relief flooded me at the sound of their voices.

"They're being burned on the inside. Something Evander injected. Ring any bells?"

No one answered, and I almost spoke again before Dane finally did. "I'm looking it up."

"Me too," Wade supplied.

Okay. I had to get more answers than this. There were things we knew about Evander. They never put a disease out to the population they couldn't cure. They had two reasons for this. The first was that they might decide eliminating a population was cutting into profits and change their minds. Second, they had to be able to cure it in case a member of the board of directors got sick. They never risked themselves.

Somewhere on this fucking ship was answers.

I was alone in the sense that I wasn't actively being watched for the first time in forever. That was fine. Brenden and Matt were doing just what I would have wanted, saving my loves. But that didn't mean I was ready to leave yet. I wouldn't be dumb. If I got into trouble, someone would have to rescue me, and I didn't want that. I wasn't sneaking anywhere.

"Guys, I'm going to find the med bay on this clunker. They must have something. See if there are answers. Tell a Z, any Z, that you see. Okay?"

There was some static but finally Wade spoke. "Careful Amber. I hear that ship is in bad shape."

He had no idea. It was a walking death trap, but it would not be the place responsible for my husbands' deaths. They were going to get to be old men. I would see to it. By sheer force alone.

The med bay was nothing more than one med machine, a table, and a shelf of drugs. They obviously cared little about saving anyone here. I disconnected the machine. I'd take it with me. Nothing was labeled. There was nothing that screamed poison to me. I would take everything with me, rolling it in the med machine.

"Amber?" Brenden came over my earpiece. "I'm coming back for you. Don't move. Not an inch. Where are you?"

"You can't see it, but I'm rolling my eyes at you. I am moving. I am taking this med machine, and I am coming to the bay to meet you there. Thank you for saving them."

He groaned. "Fine. Don't move from the..."

I didn't hear what he said because as I flipped open the lid of the med machine to stick everything I couldn't carry in it, I found a man. Hiding.

We stared at each other for a second. He wore a white lab coat, the universal sign of medical professional, and as he registered my awareness of him, fear crossed his features, and he paled.

"I didn't want to."

No good conversation ever started like that. "You didn't want to what?"

"I didn't want to inject them. I never want to inject people. They... they make me."

This man had injected my husbands, and he was going to hide in the med machine until we went away? I grabbed a scalpel from the shelving unit, one of the few tools there. "I know how to use this thing. What is your name?"

His voice shook. "Todd Anderson, I'm a medic."

All right. He didn't make the medicine, but he knew how to administer it. I didn't know how it worked with Evander, but here we all took oaths to do no harm. They might have made him do these things, but I was afraid he'd find that I had no sympathy.

"Congratulations, Todd Anderson. You have just earned yourself a trip to the Chen Empire. Whether you live to get out of there will be entirely up to you." The door behind me swung open. Brenden was out of breath. Whatever problem he would have given me for not being where I'd said I would died on his lips when he saw the scene before him. "This is Master Brenden." They were all Masters when spoken about to Outsiders. I'd picked that up somewhere. "Master Brenden, this man injected everyone with whatever Evander did to them. I stepped back. Keep him alive long enough to talk."

My guard nodded once. "Understood."

I might have been just a tad bit fine with pain when it came to revenge. Maybe more than fine with it. For the first time ever, I felt like a Chen.

"I think it was the green vials and that is pretty much what that man said before he started screaming again." Dane stared at the bottle in front of him. "This is the one for sure. It's a virus, and as far as the machines can tell it eats the victim from the inside out. Tears at the tissue. It's... painful. To say the least. They experimented with it on a Dark Planet. Help got there and with assistance it has a fifty percent mortality rate."

My whole body went cold. I walked to the running med machines. With no idea what we were dealing with quite yet, all of the patients, including my husbands, had been put into the machines and told them to give us a readout on what we were looking at. We knew the pathogen they'd been injected with now.

As I stared at the too pale forms of my beloveds, Dane entered the information on the toxin into the machine. Now, we'd find out what we could do. If anything. I rubbed my arms. Fifty percent wasn't high enough.

The Z gathered in the hall outside. I was going to have to tell them something about their leaders.

"How long a stretch in the machines did those who lived have?" I could look it up myself but I suspected Dane knew that off the top of his head. We'd stayed on Artemis with Wade and all the patients. Melissa piloted Malice, ahead of us, in case we ran into trouble.

We'd taken down a fleet ship of Evander but there were bound to be more. At least two more if Blaze's instincts were right.

Sienna stayed in the corner, monitored by all of us from the silence of her med machine.

She was silent, no touching of my brain right now. Wade moved between the machines, taking readouts.

"Someone beat the shit out of Shane." Wade shook his head. "He must really have pissed them off."

I nodded. What would have been said or what happened to make the sweetest of my husbands drive his captors to beat him like that?

"Amber, I hate to tell you how long it's going to be," Dane spoke softly. "You've had enough."

I shook my head. "Just lay it on me, Dane. I'm as tough as I have to be."

"It could be up to a year."

Wade winced. That was a long stretch. No wonder there was such a high mortality rate. Some people just couldn't exist in the machine for that long. They weren't meant to keep us alive endlessly when we were meant to die. That was the sad truth of it. The machines could perform miracles, but our bodies had to have fight left in them to do so.

Some doctors took patients who were on extend care like that out for a while, kept them in a medically induced comatose state, but brought them outside to feel the sunshine, hear voices, breathe fresh air. I didn't see any evidence of that helping anything.

I stiffened my back. "Well, they'll have to be strong. They promised me."

I was going to hold onto that like a deranged person if I needed to. I squared my shoulders. It was time to go tell the Z.

"Not so fast," Dane stopped me. "I've been running a scan on you while I do this."

I sighed. The old-fashioned doctors were fantastic because they had a life of knowhow behind them. Dane could probably deliver a baby while steering the ship and fixing himself a drink. But they didn't care about privacy. He should have asked me first.

"And?" I supposed I should have been grateful he'd done this. "Something wrong?"

"Your blood pressure is once again borderline. I don't like it. Particularly with twins."

I put my hand on my hips. "Dane, my husbands are lying near death. Poisoned. Evander's manipulations eating them from the inside out like some kind of parasite. Give me a second to pull my anxiety down."

"You're on bed rest."

I blinked. "What?"

"You're on bed rest. And you can't argue or look at Wade. I outrank him."

Wade scrunched up his face. "We have ranks?"

"I'm on bed rest?" It was almost never used, ever. "Well, I've got news for you. I'm not going on bed rest. My husbands are in here. This is where I plan to be."

He nodded. "I thought you might say that. But this is Artemis, and I know her better than I know my room on Mars Station. I lived in this room for years. So I know that from the wall there is an attached ottoman."

Wade whirled around. "There is?"

"It's well hidden. The designer of this ship was very interested in stealth. You are going to sit on it with your feet up and do things like read or redesign the layout of the Chen Empire. You aren't going to run on ships or send your energy bellowing through space. On that ottoman. Now."

I swallowed. I wanted to take care of the babies. I wasn't going to argue. "For how long?"

"Until I tell you otherwise. Now, go tell the Z what they need to know and then come back and sit down. This also means you aren't torturing anyone for information. The Z don't need you to do that. It is possible to not micromanage everything. That's a hard lesson I had to learn. You, too, Wade. You don't have to run the universe."

My shoulders sagged. "Dane, if they live through this, if they stay in those machines for a year, then we will be apart just about as long as we were when I ran from them. They will miss the birth of the babies. And... I don't know how I can do this alone."

His face softened. "You'll do it because you're full of wonders and so much more than you even know you are. I've known you since you were a little girl. You are a survivor. The world spins around you, it gets out of control. Chaos takes over. And somehow you make order of it. Just when it seems like all is lost, you fix it. That's what you do, Amber. Paloma made scenes. You created order. It wasn't weakness. It was strength beyond the likes of which your sister could understand back then. Your parents didn't see. I did. Someone else might break. You never will."

C.J. leaned against the doorway. "I'd listen to him. When he makes speeches, he tends to be right."

I nodded. "Thank you, Dane."

Wade lifted his head. "I never had anyone in my life ever talk to me like that."

C.J. patted him on the back. "Stick around this crew and stop hiding in your room. Someone is bound to say something profound to you eventually. We can't seem to help ourselves."

━━━

I leaned on the ottoman, a medical tablet in my hand, and

tried to read about Evander diseases without wanting to throw up.

Kelton entered the med bay and came up to me. He knelt. "I wanted to get your opinion on some things. I'm sending instructions back to Chen to start rebuilding. If we don't have your husbands for maybe up to a year, we have to get started without them. I'm trying to see things as they would. So of course we need to rebuild the mansion."

I hated that place. The ostentatious mansion that housed my mother-in-law, her ilk, and the beatings I'd taken. The whole of Chen Empire needed a makeover. I blinked. Yes, it did. A big old changeover.

I was in charge. Could I... fix things?

"Kelton." I stopped him. "I'm going to disagree with you. And I know it may not be how my husbands would see things. I know that makes it complicated for you, but here is how I see it. We don't need that mansion. Why bother? It's taking up space better used for other things. Build us a house. A big enough one for me, the kids, my husbands, and guests. Let's assume a few more kids. We can always use the space for something else if we want later. A big house, not a mansion. Put it on the outskirts of the living area for Chen Central. A nice view." There were some things I'd splurge on. The Masters Chens deserved some perks for the things they did.

He rapidly blinked. "What do you propose to do with the space the mansion took up?"

"We need to rebuild Earth. Right now, I see a three-fold problem. First, the orphans. There have to be a ton of them all over Earth. They need to be housed and fed and cared for. Take half the space of the mansion and build an orphanage. The goal is to find them good homes. I want an extreme screening process. We can get to that later."

Kelton grinned. "I love that. What else?"

"We need to update the medical facilities. I want a real hospital. Not just because I want it for me. I want it for all of us. We shouldn't have to go elsewhere for medical help and should we find ourselves in another war I don't want anything makeshift."

Kelton nodded so I continued.

"Oceania is gone. Chen Empire needs to be the center of commerce. Build us a place for that. And let it be known that whoever wants to build their business in Chen will find us very accommodating to new businesses. I think if Amari were here, he'd agree with that. How can he be the best businessman alive if there is nowhere to do that? All of this as we preserve the water and leave space for Hunter to impose his own designs."

Kelton rose. "We're all lucky to have you, Amber. I didn't think of any of this."

"Kelton, a fourth problem. I don't ever want another fucking attack. Get Hunter's team working on it. It won't be ready until he can design it himself, but damn it, I want Earth to be so protected that assholes like Evander wouldn't fucking dare."

He grinned. "Yes, ma'am."

WHY WAS it whenever I wanted time to speed up, it dragged, and when I wanted it to slow down, it flew? These were the kind of thoughts plaguing me in the endless days of waiting. My blood pressure normalized, and by the time the Z finished construction on our non-palace-y house, there was snow on the ground. I'd forgotten how beautiful the snow could be in the Chen Empire.

My breath fogged up the window, and I sipped my tea, feeling my babies move inside of me. Twins almost always came early. I probably didn't have much time left until they joined us. As it was, I had come to discover that one of them was a lot more active than the other. I wondered if that would translate outside of the womb.

"I think we've gotten everything we can get from him," Kelton told me, and I turned around. "It might be time to finish with Todd."

He said his name with derision, and I smiled. "Send him on his way. Drop him somewhere in the middle of space, on a reforming station, and let him tell the entire world what treatment you get if you fuck with the Chen Empire."

Kelton's eyes widened. "I thought we'd just kill him, but that works, too."

I sighed and walked up to him. "Leave him alone for a few weeks. Deal with it after your honeymoon. "I grinned at him. It was going to be a wonderful day for him. "Your tie isn't straight."

Dane had let me off bed rest weeks earlier and it was nice to be up and moving. I adjusted Kelton's tie. It was purple, like the sash the Z always carried with them. If Amari had been well, he'd have been doing this ceremony. As it was, they'd ask Cooper to perform it. He was stunned, but the entire Z Warriors had taken to him over the last few months as he'd helped them redesign the entire agricultural set up in the fifth quadrant.

Everyone would be leaving soon.

Evander wasn't gone, but they were hidden in the Dark Planets. That meant that my friends and family would head in that direction. Rebuilding The Farm was a smart move since its location was so much closer to the Dark Planets. The unmarried Super Soldiers headed into the Dark Planet area to search. Blaze had taken Artemis and continued to hide Sienna with the same shipmates who had been with him before.

We heard nothing from them, which Melissa said was a good sign.

Brenden and Chrissy had gotten married the week before. At all of these things I put on my best fake smile and pretended to be joyful while in my head there was a constant countdown. The fifty percent was playing out. So far, of the twenty-five people rescued, twelve still lived, including my three guys.

I rubbed the back of my neck. This morning, they had strong brain waves, even Shane, who I'd obsessed over for weeks because of his head injuries, and their vitals were good. But for how much longer?

Still, I smiled. This was Kelton's wedding day, and I was the Chen wife. I would be what everyone needed me to be: happy.

"Don't rework the map of Earth while I'm on Saturn's rings. You don't have to fix everything yourself."

I cleared my throat. "The babies move around all night, I can't sleep. I need something to do with my time. Why not alter everything at the same time?"

"Funny."

I straightened his tie again. "Go get married, Master Kelton. I won't change a thing while you and Matt are away."

He nodded. "They'll be up soon. They're strong, hanging on, and Dane said their vitals are steady. It's working."

"True." Except they all looked that way, every patient in there seemed fine. Until the day they died.

―――

I sat with my tablet in my hand, reading about nursing strategies while Dane checked on all of the patients. Lewis and Cash would be leaving today, now that the wedding festivities were over.

"Dane," I caught his attention as Ari entered the room. "Are you leaving?"

He shook his head. "Not until everyone here is okay. They're my patients."

Ari pointed at me. "And I'm delivering those babies. So... you're stuck with me, too."

I should have expected the tears that came. "Thank you."

I wiped them away and no one commented, which I appreciated. There were very good doctors on Earth, but I didn't know them like I did these men. I would have to figure it out, and as for my own career, it was pretty much stalled since I wasn't allowed on my feet the amount I needed to be. Funny enough, at the moment, I didn't miss it. I was sure there would come a time I would. But managing my constant anxiety and staying healthy for the babies was about all I could do at the moment.

It wasn't a great truth but there it was.

"You didn't think we were going to leave you, did you Amber? Paloma's not going anywhere either. Diana and her crew are just going to get set up. If you needed Cash and Lewis here, they'd stay, too." Dane turned around to speak to me.

I touched my stomach. "I'm a little off today."

Dane smirked at me, and I knew what he was going to ask before he did. "Can I scan you?"

I'd finally gotten him to the point where he was asking permission, resentfully. "Sure."

He hit a button, and I didn't look up while he read whatever readouts he saw. "You're doing fine."

I kind of figured that. "Just the pregnancy hormones, I guess."

An alarm sounded seconds before a loud bang shot the lid off Amari's med machine. I jumped up in time to see my oldest husband leap from the machine. His eyes were wild.

I somehow managed to get my eyes to his scanner. His brain waves didn't show alertness. This was my husband, the greatest Z Warrior, who had been under sedation for seven months, breaking his med machine and basically sleep walking himself into a violent state.

"No one move," I yelled to the room as three Z rushed in. "I mean it. Not one of you."

He was lethal, and he wasn't awake.

I loved this man, and I wasn't afraid of him, not for me.

He strode toward Dane, and I wondered what he saw, who he saw. The last time he'd been awake he'd been tortured, injected with a poison virus he still battled, and I wasn't confident he wasn't about to kill someone in a dream state that showed him he was still there. I'd monitored his brain waves for nightmares but that wasn't one hundred percent accurate. He might not have been having one, he might have just been seeing what happened over and over. Those readings would be different.

"Amari," I said his name, and he stopped mid-stride. It should have been impossible to break his machine the way he'd done. I'd heard stories of it happening once in a million times, but even the Super Soldiers stayed under when they were in it. Those Z brain waves were just different. All of that energy training altered things.

I said his name again. "Amari, it's Amber."

He stared at me but I wasn't sure he saw me. Still, something registered.

"Be careful," Ari called out to me, and I ignored him. The other doctor had a syringe in his hand. He was ready to drive that thing into Amari's neck and knock him out. I didn't want to do that. My husband's body had been through enough.

I took his hand instead, and I squeezed. Amari's unclear eyes stared down at our linked fingers.

"Amari." I drew him close to me, and he let me. If he hadn't wanted to budge, he wouldn't have. "It's Amber."

I put my arms around him and held on. This close to him, I could hear that his breathing was deep, the way he sounded when he slept, not the quick in and out of Amari alert. Yes, this was a waking dream, a nightmare for him. He just needed to be relaxed, and we could put him back under.

"Everyone out," Dane told the room. "Give her a minute. She's safe."

Ari followed Dane out the door, the nurses hustling along with them. The Z were last to leave, and I was glad that they did. I didn't want them seeing Amari like this. They would tell stories of how he broke the med machine, and they would become legends. What happened after was no one's business.

I stood there with my husband, listening to him breathe. It was that long, deep sound I craved. For a second I might even have been able to pretend we were alone in a bed, him next to me, with nothing wrong in the world. Of course, we'd never once had that moment. All of my times with my husbands had been rushed. There had been no easy days between us.

I would see to it that changed.

"Amari." I kept saying his name because it felt nice to do so. He put his head down on my shoulder, and I shuddered. I loved this. He needed to be back in the machine, but I would take this second. "You're home, and you're safe."

He nodded against my shoulder. "Home."

"That's right. You're home. And you're spending time in the med machine getting better. You just broke out because you're sleeping." I kissed his cheek. He was slightly too warm, but we'd known that. They'd all had a little bit of a fever this whole time. "And I'm going to need you to go back in."

He lifted his head. His eyes weren't clear. They wouldn't be during this exchange. People didn't just wake up from med machines, they had to ease to alertness, from real sleep to being awake outside of the machine. Particularly when they'd been in the machine as long as he had.

"I want to stay with you."

I kissed his lips gently. He wasn't contagious. "I want that, too. Only you have to get well first. So come with me." I squeezed his fingers and led him to a different machine. "You're home. You're safe. Everyone is safe. I need you to do something for me. I need you to not fight the machine, I need you to let yourself really sleep. When you wake up again, it'll all be over, and we can spend some time just being."

He shuddered. "Okay."

"Thank you." I kissed him one more time and helped him climb into the machine. Before I let it shut around him, I ran my hands through his dark hair. "Sleep for me."

"Love you, Amber." His voice was low as his eyes drifted shut.

"I love you, too."

I closed the machine and turned it on. All the med machines in here were coded for this pathogen. It would know what to do for him.

Dane stood in the doorway. "Holy shit."

I didn't turn. I needed a second. "They're very powerful. When I tell people, they don't really understand until they see it themselves."

"Have you given any thought to how strong your children are going to be?"

A warm water hit my legs and my feet. I stared down. What was happening? Was I peeing myself?

I turned to face Dane as realization hit me. "My water just broke."

He nodded. "Okay. Then it's time. Maybe he knew. That's why he came out today to speak to you, even if he didn't know that he knew. If he's that tuned into things that he can rouse himself from a med machine and destroy it? Add to that he managed to do that so fast the machine never registered that he was getting alert enough to do that? Maybe he knew."

Maybe he did. I shivered. "I'm pretty terrified right now."

"All new mothers are." After saying that, he called over his shoulder to the hallway. "Ari, get in here or I'm saying screw it and I'm delivering the babies."

Ari rushed through the door. "It's time?"

"It's time."

I was pretty sure that the entirety of the Z Warriors waited outside the door when my daughters wailed into the world. They'd both been breach, premature, and there had never been any chance I was going to try to deliver them naturally.

With my sister chatting nervously by my head, Ari numbed me and cut them from my womb, bringing them into the world.

I had a chance to stare at their faces before we were all put in med machines to get better. They were the most beautiful sight I'd ever beheld. Dark hair like their father and uncles, Shane's shape of his face, the strong Chen chin.

My eyes. I could see that right away. They had the violet blue eyes. The gene I'd inherited that was so rare it didn't show up every generation in my family. They both had it. The girls weren't identical, we knew that beforehand, but they resembled each other a great deal.

"What are their names?" Paloma stroked my hair as I stared at them, trying to memorize their faces. We would be away from each other until their bodies were a little bit stronger. I was so sick of losing my loved ones to the machines.

Maybe I wasn't thinking coherently, but I was too far gone to care.

"Josephine and Katherine. I think they'll be strong names for later. For now, they can be Josie and Katie."

Paloma kissed my forehead. "Good names. Who is who?"

"Katie was baby A the whole time she was in my belly. She was born first. Her face is a little bit longer and..."

Paloma interrupted me. "She looks a little bit more like you."

I didn't think either of them outside of their eyes resembled me but I wasn't going to argue with her.

"They're beautiful, and I love them." Paloma sniffed as Ari took them from my view.

I didn't really remember much that happened after that. It was my own turn in the machine. I decided to just go with it.

There had never been such protected babies in the history of the universe. Katie and Josie had ten guards each. They were constantly outside of the cottage. Not that they could help with the screaming, what I suspected was colic, or the constant state of being awake that happened inside. I didn't know what day it was or how many weeks old they were anymore. Six? Yes, I thought it was six.

Truth was there was nothing to do but survive this. Katie ate more than Josie but Josie nursed for longer. When one would sleep, which wasn't very often—they both seemed to want to be alert all the time—the other would wake up. It was like they were on constant watch for me. Maybe they thought that one of them had to be awake for my sake.

My cat, Applesauce, had officially retreated to hiding in the back of the house. He did not care for the screaming and after checking out the girls when they'd first come home he'd wanted next to nothing to do with them. In my few free moments, he rubbed against me to tell me he was home and otherwise left us alone.

I wasn't sleeping more than two hours a day, and I kind of thought I might have been about to crack.

I hadn't been to see my husbands in too long. Not that they would know, but I knew. I just couldn't get out of the house.

There were people who wanted to help, but I'd locked them out. I knew Paloma would be there in a second, only she had her own babies, and other than her I was feeling very protective of who saw the girls. Maybe because their own father and uncles hadn't yet.

A knock sounded. The third one that morning. Brenden and Matt were getting pushy. I thought they might think all of the baby screaming in here meant I was dead. Katie was having a particularly difficult morning.

I'd scanned her twice. There was nothing physically wrong with either of them. They gained weight. They ate.

They were healthy. And angry at the world. Or maybe they just didn't like the mother they'd been saddled with.

I shook my head. That kind of thinking wasn't helpful.

I swung open the door. Brenden tilted his head to stare at me. "Chrissy says I have to pretty much demand you let me hold the baby so that you can take a shower. And eat something."

I sighed. "Brenden, she's just going to scream the whole time."

"Fine, then she screams. That's Katie, right?" He stepped inside. "Hard to tell from behind. They have the same hair color. I will let the Z heir scream at me for half an hour while you take a shower. I won't drop her. I won't..."

We were interrupted as two Z appeared next to him. They were the girls' currently scheduled guards. One of them spoke. "I'll hold Katie. She's my charge, and I'm good with babies."

I wanted to throw something. "I appreciate the help but..."

This time Brenden interrupted me. "We're all family. Okay? The Z is family. It goes beyond family. I know you understand this. I know you can feel it. Their father is our family and more. You are, too. They are. And you are falling apart. Let me take her. You don't know these two well enough yet. They'd lay down their lives, but you don't know it yet and..."

All of this stopped as two more Z arrived. I gasped. They held up Hunter in their arms, who stumbled with them, eyes closed.

"What the hell?" I shouted, stepping outside.

"He's stable. Dane says he can wake up at home. I think he thinks that might go better than having him rouse, pissed off, in the med bay, considering what happened with

Amari," the Z whose name was Cliff told me. "Bring him to his room?"

"Yes." I moved aside. Why hadn't Dane called me? Screaming baby on my shoulder, I grabbed my tablet. I hadn't checked it in days. Dane had let me know the machine said Hunter was stable and he concurred.

"Dr. Chen." The use of my title by Brenden startled me.

I raised an eyebrow. "Really?"

"Master Hunter is back. I'm thinking we might have to all get back to the formal. Give me the baby. Before Josie wakes up. Sorry, Miss Josie, wakes up. Go see to Hunter. I won't drop her."

Katie's guard objected again, but I passed her to Brenden, who didn't drop her, as he promised he wouldn't. She lifted her head to regard him for a second, stopping her cries, before she resumed them again.

She really was angry with the world. Brenden was right. We were family. Just some of us more distant than others. I trusted him with my daughters, but he was on the short list. My shoulder felt lighter, it had been a long time since I wasn't carrying someone.

"She has to start trusting us, Brenden," Katie's guard objected. "You know it. I know it. And Master Hunter will want that."

Brenden laughed. "These are her babies, Harry. She never thought she'd have them, went through hell to keep them, more pain when they were born, and she's been essentially alone when you add it all up for years now. I'm not telling Dr. Chen who gets to hold them. Back off or I'll have you removed. Yes, I can do that."

I left the room, following Hunter. It was good to have friends. Hunter lay on the bed, his eyes closed. Cliff handed me a tablet, and I scanned Hunter's vitals. They were good. He was just out cold. This was happening.

My hand shook as I passed it back to Cliff. I'd wanted this more than anything and now I didn't know what to do.

"Amber, you have your hands full out there. Stan and I will stay until he rouses enough to eat and we're sure he's okay. No one expects you to do all of this alone."

I nodded. "Give me a minute."

Cliff backed off, Stan right by him. "We'll be in the hall."

"Thank you."

I tiptoed toward Hunter. I probably didn't need to be quiet. We'd just been talking loud enough that if he was going to really wake up he'd have done so. I smoothed the hair off his forehead. He was okay. A lump formed in my throat, and I tried to swallow through it.

He was home. Finally.

All I wanted to do in the world was curl up next to him, sleep, until he woke up, hold his body next to mine. Hopefully there would be time for that soon. So I kissed him as gently as I could. "Welcome home, Hunter. Thank you for keeping your promise."

It was a rare moment that I had both girls breastfeeding at the same time but tonight they'd both wanted to together. I actually loved it because it meant they'd, hopefully, sleep a stretch at the same time.

Hunter hadn't roused, and it was approaching midnight. That was normal. Somewhere in the back of my tired brain, I knew that. Maybe if the girls did actually sleep, I could lie down with him for a stretch. I'd ask the guards outside to stand next to their room and wake me in case I didn't hear them cry.

I could do that. I could. I'd let them in that far.

What was wrong with me?

"I can do it." Hunter's voice echoed down the hall. "I appreciate the offer but I am fine. Where is she? I'm going alone."

The tears started before he ever entered the room. Just seeing him stand in the doorway was such a gift. I couldn't speak, couldn't manage to form words.

He didn't say anything either. What did he see? Me, a wreck with no shower since Katie had been crying so loud I couldn't possibly leave her, looking like death warmed over, completely not knowing what the hell I was doing, crying on the couch?

My middle husband walked toward me, slowly. He sat down beside me, still having not said a word. "This much time has passed?"

I nodded, and he wiped the tears streaming down my face before he bent to kiss my tears.

"Who are these beauties?" Hunter cupped the back of Josie's head. The girls were both basically asleep attached to my breasts.

I forced myself to speak. "This is J-Josie." And there was the stutter. "And this is Katie. Josephine and Katherine."

Hunter kissed my cheek. "Have you been alone?"

Leave it to Hunter to get to the heart of things. "Well, I'm never alone, right? The Z are very attentive."

He shook his head. "That's not what I meant."

"Yes, I've been alone. Shane and Amari are alive, but still being treated. You woke up today. Sorry, yesterday. It's been about eight months."

Hunter winced. "I'm so sorry, my love."

"No, don't be sorry. You're alive. That's a big thank you from me. I love you. I've missed you..."

Katie cried out, and I sucked back my tears. "They're not happy babies right now. Paloma says Benjamin wasn't either for months but that doesn't make it any easier, currently."

"No, not when there are two of them." He held out his hands. "I love you, too. I want to hear all your stories. That's your expression, and I'm stealing it. Every one of your stories. Hand me one. If she's done?"

Well, Katie had stopped sucking and wasn't asleep. "She's going to cry."

"That's okay." I gently passed him Katie. She lifted her head to regard him like she had done with Brenden but didn't follow the examination with a wail. Instead, they silently stared at each other. Hunter finally laid kisses all over her face.

He spoke to her softly. "I love you. We're going to figure out how to be good to your mother, together. How I can help you get what you need and see to it that she starts to get what she needs, too."

I detached sleeping Josie from me and laid her on my shoulder. Hunter put his arm around me, drawing me to him and I went, leaning my head against him. Katie nuzzled down on Hunter's chest. This was happening. We were having a quiet moment and Hunter was here.

I couldn't keep my eyes open.

HUNTER

It was Amber's soft snore that alerted me that she'd conked out. I gently took Josie from her. I'd gone from never holding babies to having two on my chest in no time flat. The quieter of the two snuggled down, making a soft baby sound when she did. I was hooked. I loved them fiercely, and I adored their mother beyond reason.

I'd been in the darkest of places but coming home to them was like visiting the light. I never wanted to leave it. I kissed Katie's head. My brothers needed to wake up and be fine. We were a family. They had to have this love, too. These girls and my woman were going to save us all.

I never cared if I was a father, I wanted to be like my uncles. They'd been so much more there for me than my own father, who only had eyes for Amari. These girls were going to know such unconditional love from me that Shane was going to accuse me of spoiling them. That was my goal. Spoil my girls. I looked at my gorgeous wife. The dark circles were evident under her eyes even in sleep.

I was going to spoil her, too. Soon, she would know what it meant to be a Chen wife. My love had yet to experience it. We'd promised her luxury and she just kept showing us she was made of steel and didn't need it. That didn't mean I wasn't going to give it to her anyway. Amber Chen was safe. I'd see to it with every cell in my body.

AMBER

I woke myself up snoring. I jerked awake, panic overtaking me. I'd fallen asleep with Josie on me. I never did that. It was too risky. Where was she? What was...

"Easy." Hunter stroked my hair. "You're okay."

I rubbed my face. He had both girls on his chest, I must have been on his shoulder, and he was reading his tablet. Alertness tried and failed to grab me.

"Did you take the baby?"

He nodded. "When you drifted off."

I shook my head, my hair falling in my eyes. "I never, ever do that. I don't sleep with them on me."

"I wasn't worried about it." Katie shifted slightly on him. "You wouldn't have dropped her."

His confidence in me went beyond my own. "I was snoring."

He nodded slowly. "You do. We all love that sound. You know that. Go back to it."

I had to think. "Hunter, you just woke up. You need rest

and food, not to take care of me and the girls. Go back to bed."

"I'm not tired. Cliff practically spoon fed me a protein bar when I woke. I've sent them home, but I suspect they're just outside. And I'm reading through all the changes you've made here, which are smart and impressive, including this house. I've only seen two rooms, but it's adorable. I'm not tired. I promise to wake you if I get to be. You should go lie down in your bed."

My bed? "I haven't seen it in six weeks. Seven, maybe."

I watched as he digested this. "Go lie down in mine."

Why weren't the girls screaming? "How long was I snoring?"

He kissed my cheek, moving Josie just slightly when he did, then my other one. "Only about half-an-hour. Not enough. Go to bed. I've got this."

I curled up against him. "I like it right here. This is not the welcome home I wanted to give you."

"It's exactly the one I would want. Trust me, I'm going to make love to you in the not too distant future. Even if we only have minutes. But right now? I want to sit here knowing you're safe, the girls are safe, that I have all of you right here near me. You're my family. They're teeny tiny, and we're bonding."

They weren't screaming on him. "They like you better than me."

He shook his head. "No. I just don't make milk for them so they figure I'm a good bed to stretch out on. I'm also not stressed, not alone, not trying to survive in utter terror that way. You're amazing, and they love you. So do I. Go to sleep."

He had been comfortable. I put my head back on his shoulder. "Sorry about the snoring."

Katie's cry woke me. I could tell which of them it was. Josie always started smaller, getting to hysterics while Kate dove right into hysterical and never looked back.

"Sorry." I jumped to my feet and took her straight off of Hunter's chest. She was a little wet and needed to be fed. Josie would be up any second and doing the same thing.

"Stop apologizing." Hunter rose slowly, still holding Josie on his chest. "Is that how long she gives you? Two hours?"

I shrugged. "That's a good stretch for her. Josie goes longer, which is nice, but then she wants to eat as Katie is done and screaming. So I get maybe half an hour if I'm lucky most of the time. They showed off for you with the two hours straight."

Hunter's whole face scrunched up. "How are you functioning?"

"Does this look like functioning to you?" I walked to Katie's room, setting her down on the changing table. Her face was red. She was wet. Wow, did she hate being wet.

Hunter followed me. "It does, actually. But you can't keep up like this. I'm going to help you. We're going to work this out."

"There's nothing to work out. Babies scream for months, sometimes years. It's just the nature of it." I hoped I sounded calm because my husband, who just got home from eight months of medical care after being abused at the hands of Evander, did not need my hysterics. "I love them. I really do." I wanted to make that clear. "I love them even though they're so hard."

He rubbed my back, staring down at Katie. "I know you do. That doesn't mean you can't say that this is difficult. You can love them and say it's challenging. Like loving us."

I looked over my shoulder as he winked at me, and I grinned. "You should give me Josie and go to bed. It has to be hitting you."

He nodded. "It is, and I want to be alert when I am in charge of the kids. They look like you, you know. They're beautiful."

I took Josie from him as I finished with Katie. "They look like Chens. Both of them are basically different versions of Shane. They got my eye color, but they are all Chen."

He shook his head. "Katie has your shape of face, that's not Shane. And Josie, the expressions are yours. She lifts up her eyes really wide like you do. And that mouth is yours."

Hunter was seeing things I wasn't. I kissed him on the lips. "Get some sleep. Close the door. Put on the fan in your room, that'll block the noise."

"Okay." He leaned over to kiss me. "I love you. I'm sorry. I'll get up to speed, fast. I'll help you. We'll do this together."

It was just nice to have him in the house.

―――

"Hey." Hunter's voice startled me in the middle of feeding Josie. I glanced up. Once again, joy that he was home filled me. "Weren't you going to sleep?"

"That was five hours ago."

He tilted his head. "No, it wasn't. Was it?" He joined me on the couch, rubbing my back. "When was the last time you got out of the house?"

"I went to see you guys in the med bay... I don't know

how long ago that was... but the girls were screaming, so we left quickly. I took them to see Ari there, too. He's their pediatrician until he leaves. Then we'll have to decide on someone else." I might have been rambling.

He moved his hand, and ran it through my hair. "I wish it was warm enough to sit outside for a while in the sun."

"You should go for a walk. Go ahead. Go enjoy yourself."

He smirked at me. That Hunter smirk that was so adorable that also meant he found what I said ridiculous. It was possible to want to both kiss him and punch him. "I'm good here. I told Cliff to tell everyone I'd emerge in a couple of weeks. Kelton sent a message saying all is well. Amari broke out of the med machine?"

"Oh, yes, the day I went into labor. That was very... startling."

He shook his head. "How the fuck did he do that?"

"I really don't know. He was basically sleep walking, but he was going to kill Dane. I talked him down, settled him, put him back in, and then my water broke."

Hunter grinned. "My older brother has always been very intense."

"Sure, because you *aren't* intense at all?"

I loved when he laughed. It really was the best sound in the world.

———

I woke up with a hand on my back. I was on a bed I didn't remember getting on. Hunter rolled me over to face him. "They're both sleeping, and I should let you sleep, but I need to kiss you. Tell me to go away."

I wrapped my arms around his neck. "I want you to more than kiss me, my love."

I hadn't been with Hunter since before the war started. "I'm sorry. This is me being totally selfish. I..."

I stopped him by kissing him hard. He moaned against me, pressing me down on the bed with all of his weight on top of me. His mouth was warm and soft. I closed my eyes. I needed this as much as I did sleep. Maybe more. This would officially be Hunter coming home to me.

We tore at each other's clothes. Not that I had much on. The constant need to be feeding the girls made a bra pointless. My t-shirt was all that covered my top. He stared down at my breasts, his eyes obviously taking in the changes that having the girls wrought on me.

Suddenly, I was self-conscious, insecurity making me soft inside. "I... I know I look..."

"Beautiful," he whispered in my ear. "You look beautiful. Skin and bones, actually. I'm going to feed you. Take care of you while you take care of them. We're going to do this, and when spring comes, it'll all be easier."

Sexier words were never spoken. We kissed until I couldn't breathe from wanting him. There was a time limit to this that matched our frantic pace. Luxurious, no time limit sex wasn't a reality right then.

Totally naked, we rubbed at each other, dry humping as our lips made love. He caressed my body, running his hands over my breasts, gently, not squeezing too hard. He stopped over my stomach. "I wish I could have seen you pregnant."

"You did. In the ship when I found you." I kissed his cheek. He smelled like Hunter, he was mine. I rubbed my cheek against him.

"My memory is foggy, but you weren't showing yet. I

mean, it would have been so sexy to see you round with the girls inside of you, all flush and glowing."

I grinned at him before I bit his neck. "I was never flush and glowing. Pregnancy was not pretty on me."

"Liar. Everything is pretty on you."

Hunter reached between us, petting my pussy before he plunged one finger inside of me. I cried out. Yes, that felt incredible to have him there but I needed more, so much more. He touched me slowly, drawing out the feeling, not rushing, despite the fact that we probably had no time.

I followed suit. He was hard, and as I stroked him, cupping his cock in my hand, he sighed against my neck. His gaze met mine as we touched each other.

"I thought I'd never be here again with you, never hold you like this."

I shook my head. "You promised me."

"I was so afraid I was going to break it and that killed me inside. I love you, Amber. Every single part of you. Forever."

I didn't want to cry, but I let the tears slip from my eyes. "I love you like that, too, Hunter. No more time apart."

He shook his head. "None. Ever."

Hunter pushed inside of me. I cried out at the invasion. It had been a long time since I'd done this and a lot of things had happened since then. He waited before he moved, doing nothing but stroking his hands down my face.

I nodded up at him. "I'm okay."

He tilted his head in the way only Hunter could. "Sure?"

"Yes."

He moved again, in and out of me, and I lifted my hips to meet his thrusts. This was heaven, this was what I'd waited for, to be connected to him again, to feel like I was his. Much sooner than I wanted it to be, I cried out in release.

Hunter wasn't done. He vibrated against me, the way I was used to when we meditated together. It was as though his energy called out for my own. I loved this man. I sent him every bit of love I had for him, from my heart to his.

He shuddered. That must have been what he needed because he came inside of me, his breath against my cheek, his heartbeat pounding against my own.

Hunter quickly gathered me up against him, kissing my face. "I'm always going to want that."

I grinned. "Even when we're old and gray?"

He laughed. "I actually didn't mean the sex. But yes," he laughed, a delicious sound in my ear, "I'm going to want sex when we're old and gray. No, I mean, I'm going to want that connection of our souls. The way you sent me your love. I need it. I think it saved me in the dark place. I hung on, waiting to hear you again and again."

I snuggled against him, back to stomach. "I wasn't sure if it was me or if it was the girls letting me do it because I carried Chen blood with them, but I could do it just now."

"It was always you, Amber. But don't you ever go boarding Evander ships again."

Smiling, I kissed his wrist and his hand before settling it on my stomach. He kissed my shoulder, the back of my neck. That was how I fell asleep, so grateful to have him home, to have his warmth against mine.

I never felt him move, but I did feel him come back with Katie as he sat down on the bed. "She's changed. I did that. Josie's still out." He kissed my forehead.

I lifted my head. "You can't know how incredible it is that you brought her to me. Thank you."

"Don't thank me for doing this very little thing. I'll stay

here with you unless Josie cries. Then I'll take Katie when she's done. And," he put a piece of toast right near my mouth, "eat that. It's just toast. The fridge is stocked with frozen food I'm guessing Paloma cooked for you. Starting tomorrow, you're eating regularly."

As I latched the baby onto my breast I stared at him. "Hunter..."

"If you say thank you, it's going to piss me off."

Well, then, I'd just think it.

I was warm, wrapped in a blanket and dozing on the couch when Amari arrived home. Or I should say when he was brought home by multiple Z guards who did little more than nod at me and escort my out-cold husband to his room. Hunter jumped up and followed Cliff, who was with Amari, from the room.

I trailed after them.

Hunter stared down at his sleeping brother. "Why weren't we informed he'd woken?"

"Like with you, Master Hunter, it was very sudden. He was totally stable and the doctor felt it was better he really wake up here."

Hunter nodded. "Any word on Shane?"

"He had a head injury." I walked over to Amari and touched his forehead. He didn't stir, but he wasn't hot like the last time I'd touched him. That was a huge relief. "The machine had to heal that. Fifty percent of the people given the drug died." I could hardly speak the words. "I've been scared for all of you. But Shane terrifies me."

Hunter kissed my cheek. "He'd never leave you. He's coming back."

I stroked my hand down his arm. "Hunter, why don't you take a break? Sit with Amari."

"You keep trying to let me out of doing what I want to be doing, which is just being with you and my girls. Cliff, stay with Master Chen."

He nodded. "That would be my pleasure, sir. Amber, don't worry. Master Shane will come back."

I felt it the second Hunter's attention zeroed in on Cliff. I whirled around, linking my arm through Hunter's. "I actually prefer them to be less formal with me. It's fine."

"It's not fine," Hunter spoke with a clenched jaw, and I dragged him from the room. I just wanted to feel relief that Amari was fine, not have this argument right now. Cliff bowed his head, very low, and I closed the door behind me.

Hunter put his hand over his chest. "We get to call you Amber. Your family gets to call you Amber. I have a hard enough time with it, but your friends get to call you Amber. The Z do not call you Amber. You are Dr. Chen. That is what they call you."

I put my arms around his neck. "We've all been through a lot together here. I am a pretty informal person. I don't mind them calling me Amber."

He made a sound that was somewhat close to a growl. "Amber. I... I... I am going to have to get used to the idea. I am going to try. I can do that. Amari is going to lose his shit."

Well, at least he was now here to do just that. I let out a breath but not all of my anxiety. Shane was still in the med machine, battling for his life. I wouldn't be okay until they were all back.

Josie cried out. At least I had a lot to keep me distracted.

———

The house was quiet. Hunter had passed out in the bed with Katie bundled up in a portable bassinet next to him on the bed. His hand was on her stomach as she lay on her back, sleeping. She'd actually gone three hours the last time she slept.

Hunter had lit a fire in the fireplace, and I stared at the flames. With Josie at my breast, it wasn't a bad moment. Amari stepped into the room so quietly I almost missed him. If he'd had an exchange with the Z, I hadn't heard it.

I sat up as much as I could. "Hi."

He padded over to me, dressed only in a loose pair of gray pants and a white t-shirt. His hair was wet. He sat down on the couch, still not having said a word. Briefly, he touched Josie's back before he sprawled and set his head on my lap.

With my free hand, I stroked his damp hair and the side of his cheek. "Hi," he finally said back, before he closed his eyes.

He sighed, his body relaxing. His breathing evened out. The shower had probably done him in for the night.

Josie finished, but I didn't move her, just letting her sleep on my chest. We'd all stay like that until morning.

———

Amari lifted his head, which woke me. I ran my hand through his hair again. It was totally dry now. Josie made little baby noises as she stirred. In the bedroom, Katie cried and it sounded like Hunter changed her diaper. He'd figured out how to do that.

My oldest husband rubbed his eyes. "Amber." His smile was huge. "I came out here to talk. I don't remember much after that. Wow. That's a baby. That much time passed?"

"I know. It's lunacy. Eight months," Hunter spoke over crying Katie as he exited the room, handing her to me and taking Josie who yawned but closed her eyes.

Amari's gaze on me made me blush as I concentrated on letting Katie latch. When I felt the familiar pull, I raised my own eyes to meet his. "Welcome home, Amari."

"I'm sorry we were gone so long."

I shook my head. "Don't apologize for getting taken. I thought you'd all died in space for about ten minutes. That was hell."

"Who are these people in our lives now?" He got up and stared at Josie in Hunter's arms. "Introduce me to my nieces. Where is Shane?"

Hunter shook his head. "Not up yet. Still waiting."

Amari made a low sound in his voice. "I don't like that."

"Give him time." I forced myself to sound optimistic. "In Hunter's arms is Ms. Josephine Chen. I call her Josie."

Hunter grinned. "I call her Ms. Josie. She demands that kind of respect."

"And hungry right now is her big sister, Katherine Chen. Or Katie."

Amari stroked Josie's head, gently. "Do you call her Ms. Katie?"

"Oh, no, she's Katherine." Hunter laughed. "Full name Katherine. Yelling Katherine. She is currently disgruntled with life. Beautiful. Ethereal. Angry. They both have Amber's violet eyes." Hunter passed me Josie who latched onto the other breast. Doing this tandem was always awkward but the payoff of them on the same schedule made it worth it.

"Welcome, beautiful girls. You are so loved." Amari kissed both of them on their cheeks. Katie stopped eating to lift her head and regard Amari the way she did all new people. As though she accepted him into her mind, she got back to feeding.

Hunter walked to Amari and bowed his head, placing it on Amari's shoulder. They stayed like that for a second before Hunter embraced him in a tight hold. The younger brother's shoulders sagged for a second. "Amari."

Amari held him as fiercely.

Not so long ago, this would have shocked me. Even when we'd first gotten back to Earth before the war, I wouldn't have understood. It wasn't until I spent time with the Z that I'd understood. Amari was more to the Z than just another Z. He was their leader and that meant more to them than just business. It was almost spiritual.

They separated, both of them turning back to me. "You know you're even more famous now, Amari. You broke out of the med machine and tried to wake up."

He put his hands on his hips. "Are you kidding?"

"Nope."

Amari slouched down on the couch. "Just one question. Where the fuck are we?"

Hunter handed him a tablet. "Our girl made some needed changes. This is where we live now. It's very nice. The perfect size. They're building an orphanage and a business area."

Amari put his hand on Josie's back. "Not ready for it yet. I'm on vacation. How did we get home?"

Hunter pointed at me. "She found us. Convinced the Z to take her to us, somehow."

Amari put my feet on his lap. "Why do you look so tired?"

Hunter laughed before he walked to the kitchen. "I'm making breakfast. Try not to stick him back in the med machine while you almost kill him."

"I don't get a lot of sleep. The girls are round the clock care, and I was alone. But Hunter has been here several days, and he is spoiling me. I feel less alone and that is somehow helpful more than anything else."

My oldest husband adored me with his eyes. "Consider yourself twice spoiled. And I am in love with this. You with those babies. You were okay? During the pregnancy?"

"I was, thanks to a really lucky design by Hunter."

Hunter walked out of the kitchen carrying pancakes. "She doesn't eat."

Between the two of them, I was fed like a toddler from a fork. It was ridiculously good. A knock sounded on the door, and Amari rose to answer it.

"Oh," Hunter shouted out. "The Z call her Amber, and she prefers it because she likes to be informal."

My husband somehow managed to open the door and gawk at me at the same time. "Well, that's stopping."

I sighed. This was going to be an ongoing problem. But we had no time for that as Shane, like his brothers before him, was helped into the house.

Hunter put his hand on my shoulder. "Don't jump up. You've got the girls. I'll settle him in."

Dane followed Shane through the door. That was different. I took one look at his face and knew he had something to tell me. "What's wrong?"

"We're going to watch Shane. He's stable. I wouldn't release him if he weren't. But there may have been permanent damage. We'll just have to see."

I swallowed. "With what?"

"His heart."

AMARI AND HUNTER went still in the way only the Chens could. I knew what that meant. They were pulling in the terror those words presented to them. I actually wasn't scared. This was medical. I could do medical. This wasn't a giant corporation bent on destroying us all.

The heart could be fixed. That was one of the beautiful things of the time we lived in.

"How bad is the damage?"

Dane shook his head. "I'm not sure. I can't find a cause on any of the scans. His heart skipped a few beats. I put him back. It did it again. Then it stopped. Maybe it's corrected. Maybe it's anomalous."

I nodded. "Maybe it's a thing now. Is he wearing a permanent heart scanner?"

"He is. Check it for him a couple times a day? Let me know. And no marathon running or anything. Not that he could do that in this snow. Unless that is also something the Chens do in the snow?"

"Dane." I had to ask it. "Your recommendation on sex? Yes? No?"

He grinned. "Yes. Check it after. Even if something went wrong, you'd handle it. You've saved more lives in this war than I did, Dr. Chen." His deliberate use of my title wasn't lost on me. "Your husbands haven't heard the stories, I imagine. But I have. You're on maternity leave, but you aren't done. If Shane needed saving, you'd do it. And I don't think it'll come to that. I sent his heart scan and the EKG to your tablet. Peruse at your leisure."

Dane exited. A second later the Z followed and would have left had I not stopped them. "Guys, it's cold out there. Go home. We don't need the permanent guard right now. Tell Brenden, Matt or whoever is mine the same as well as the girls'."

"Amber," Cliff sighed. "That's our role. We guard the Chens."

Amari jolted and then looked at Hunter. "I thought you were kidding."

I ignored them. "Send Brenden in. I'll take this up with him. I have two conscious Z with me. The girls are safe. If the satellites suddenly show incoming disaster, come and get the girls and save my husbands. I won't object. Go. Now. Please."

He sighed, but he left. "I'm not sending in Brenden. I'll just tell him to go home and that it came from you. He'll grumble and go."

I closed the door.

Amari had a hand over his left eye. I stared at him for a second. "Headache?"

He dropped his hand. "I'm going to put aside what just happened there for a hot minute."

I patted his arm before I kissed it. He shuddered at my touch. "Good. You want to know about Shane. He's going to be fine. There might be some small damage to his heart.

The drug you were given attacked your vital organs. His might have been hurt. But he'll be okay. We'll fix it, whatever it is."

Amari nodded. "Okay. I... I am going to lie down. I feel like an old man."

I touched his arm. "It's just the drugs."

He pointed at me. "We're not done with the whole being addressed as Amber thing."

I leaned up to kiss him, and he stilled before he kissed me back, so gently. "Okay, Amari. We can talk about it later. I love you. You can't know how it feels to have you back. I wasn't whole without you."

He stroked the side of my cheek. "Amber, I'm going to make you so happy." Katie took that moment to wail loudly. He looked down at her. "And you, as well, little loud one and your quieter sister. We're all going to be so happy."

I decided to believe him.

—

"Every night? They have her up like this *every* night?" Amari's voice drifted into the room, reaching me despite the fact that I paced the back of the house with two screaming babies in my arms.

I shook my head. Amari couldn't order this away. I kissed Katie's head. "I don't think you're angry, Katie. I think you're confused. I think you don't know what has rocked your world, and you are just going to yell about it until you do. I bet you'll be happy when you can sit up, when you can crawl, when you have some control over yourself. That's a Chen personality."

Hunter laughed in the doorway. "Because you have no need to control your surroundings?"

All right, he had me there. "Maybe you got it from both sides."

"They're fed. They're not wet. Hand me one. Hand Amari the other." I gave Josie to Hunter.

Holding her close, he walked over to the window. "Let's go look at the snow through the window."

Amari approached slowly, like he might do with a wounded animal. Which one of us did he think was about to attack? Me or the eight-week-old baby?

"You don't have to take her."

He put out his arms. "I don't have that much experience with babies."

"Neither did I," Hunter said without turning around. "But just throw yourself into it and don't drop her. It'll be fine."

Amari nodded seriously. "I would never drop her. Someone would have to kill me first."

"Well, hopefully it won't come to that." I handed her to Amari. He slipped her against his shoulder. She was tired. I could see it from the way she rubbed her face against him. Why did she battle sleep so hard?

"Go to sleep, Amber." Hunter turned from the window. "Or eat one of the hundred frozen meals Paloma has for you in the fridge. Or take a shower. Just take a break."

"Maybe we could all just sit here together. I realize it's not all that pleasant with the screaming." Josie had actually stopped, so hopefully Katie wasn't too far behind. "That's what I'd really like to do."

Hunter nodded before he sat on the couch. Amari followed suit, and I snuggled in between them. A few minutes later, Katie stopped.

"You know," Amari kissed her head and then my cheek, "I thought we were all dead on that ship. That was it. And when I think about potentially missing this... I can't stand it."

I leaned my head on his shoulder. "I can't think about that at all. And you like it? Even with the screaming?"

"They're just spirited. That will be good for them later." He sounded so sure. I loved how Amari made up his mind about things and then somehow willed that into existence. He grinned. "If they're still screaming like this at ten, I'll have words with them."

I must have closed my eyes.

———

"You're up."

Amari's voice woke me, and I lifted my lids to see Shane standing in the doorway of the living room. He rubbed his eyes. "I think a lot of time has passed." He touched his chest. "And I have this cool monitor on me now that I also think is not a fashion thing. And you two are holding my daughters. So maybe more time than I even realized. Hi, Amber." His voice broke. "I missed you."

I rushed at him and threw my arms around him. This was it. They were all finally *here*.

"I missed you, too." I breathed him in. "It's a heart monitor. You're going to be fine. Don't worry."

He wiped my tears away with his thumbs. "Amber. I heard your voice. Right before it all went black, and I remember thinking that it would be a great last thing to hear. You were... able to talk to us. Somehow. Through the energy. And I thought I could die because I'd heard you again."

I lost it. I'd never really understood that expression before but there it was. All of the angst exploded out of me, and took my knees out with me. I would have hit the floor if Shane hadn't grabbed me.

"Fuck." Hunter jumped up, still holding the baby. "Don't say that to her. She hasn't slept in two months."

"I..." Shane kissed my face, holding me against him. "I'm sorry. I didn't mean I wanted to. I hung on. I did. We're all here. Fuck."

I had to find my voice. "Not your fault. I'm sorry."

Shane walked to Amari, and like I'd seen Hunter do, pressed his head down on my oldest husband's shoulder. It was some kind of acknowledgement that he'd returned, that he was back with Chen. Maybe it was an apology. I didn't know exactly, I just knew it was beautiful. After a long moment, Amari hugged him—one handed since he held Katie on one shoulder.

Hunter strode toward them, slightly elbowing Shane with a grin.

"Here, take your daughter. This is Josie." Hunter passed sleeping Josie to Shane who suddenly looked like he'd been stunned silent. He stared down at her. The sight was so funny, his eyes wide, his brow furrowed, that it knocked the tears right out of me.

Amari placed Katie on Shane's shoulder. "Here you go, Daddy."

Hunter held me against him. Oh, how I'd wanted just this moment. "Sorry, guys, I'll pull it together. I'm not sad. Not really. Just overwhelmed."

Amari took my hand. "And exhausted. Sleep a little bit more while they do."

That sounded like a good idea.

Babies don't scream every two hours forever. As months passed, I was extremely relieved by that fact. Eventually, both of the girls stopped being so full of angst. Katie regularly laughed and charmed the heck out of everyone who came near her while Josie was more reticent but happy to be around her family.

They slept through the night just about the time the snow melted outside and spring pushed its way into our lives once more.

I stared at Shane's heart monitor. "Not a blip."

"It is beating, right?" He winked at me. "I mean, I do have a heart. I know I do. You own it."

I kissed his lips, and he grinned at me. "You do and the readings are good. I'm thinking we can get this taken off you soon."

As if on cue, the door to the house buzzed and Brenden poked his head in. "Melissa and Dane are here."

We'd been mostly left alone for months. With everything being rebuilt, Hunter had to interfere a few times to fix up design flaws but had otherwise really not returned to work. Amari ran things from his tablet a few times a day, and Shane had checked the water locally but not flown off to do anything outside of our little area.

I hadn't gotten back to work. I still didn't like to leave the girls, and it was even hard for me to bring myself to take them from the house very much.

As it warmed up, Shane insisted on walks around what he called the village, so the girls went in their strollers. They looked around with their violet eyes wide as they chewed on their toys and their hands.

There wasn't a person in the Chen Empire who didn't stop to admire and speak to them. Katie ate it up and Josie tolerated it, pretty well.

I still didn't like to leave them with anyone other than my husbands. Amari had suggested a nanny. Once. And then not again.

"Let them in." I smiled at Brenden before I looked down to make sure I was actually dressed. Half the time I didn't know if I was wearing a bra or if I had baby spit up on me somewhere. That my husbands regularly wanted me naked and in their beds really spoke to the fact that they must love me and somehow still see me as sexy.

I'd showered that morning. I could probably see visitors.

Melissa grinned at me as she came through the door. "You look so much better than the last time I saw you."

She'd been by to see the girls a few times. "How long ago was that?"

Melissa threw her head back and laughed. "New motherhood. I was running through an ice planet with baby Diana. I don't remember those days, and it's not because of brain damage. I just don't remember them."

Dane shook his head. "You do look well."

Amari rounded the corner from the kitchen. "Hello."

There was a real discrepancy between the Chen Empire visiting and my friends. No one bowed when Amari walked in the room if they'd come from elsewhere. He didn't seem to mind. "How are you guys? Everything okay?"

Dane nodded before he grinned at Shane. "Came to take away the heart monitor. You had one weird reading in the beginning but not since. So I'm going to say you're safe."

"Thanks." Shane winked at me again. "I just needed to get my heart back to its true owner."

I shook my head but grinned at him. "He's so sweet."

"And I'm here to tell you guys we're leaving."

I'd known that had to be coming, but still it made my own heart clench. Waverly and her crew would be next.

Diana. Damian. Sterling. Cash. Lewis. Judge. Melissa. Dane. C.J. Cooper. Nolan. Wes. Geoff. They were all going to be gone.

I touched her arm. "Are you following your daughter back to the Farm?"

"No, actually. I fully expect Waverly to go there soon. But we are retaking Mars Station. No one can find the two Evander ships in the Dark Planets. That's very concerning and the majority of the Super Soldiers have headed out there to deal with that. We think the best use of our resources is to reopen Mars Station, considering its close-ness to the Black Hole. We can help facilitate their exit through it if they manage not to get killed and make sure no one else comes through to help them. Plus, if an all-out war breaks out again we're close by."

Amari nodded and Hunter came down the hall. "Makes sense. We can regroup and come out to join the fight in the Dark Planet quadrant."

"I knew you'd say that and I've come to say don't do that."

Hunter picked up Josie from where she played on the floor. "Don't do it? Half the fleet was Z. You don't think we need to participate. I want those fuckers out of this side of the galaxy right now. I don't want them near my children, my wife, my empire. I want them gone."

Amari smirked. "He speaks for all of us."

"We want that, too. And on that note, we need you to get Earth ready. I know plans were started, but I don't think they've progressed because everyone wanted all three of you to be involved. So if you could maybe do that." She rubbed her arms. That had to be uncomfortable to say. She was basically asking us to pull our shit together and get back to things. It was time. She was right. "And there's something else."

Shane watched her from where he still sat on the floor. "What's that?"

"There is a ship headed here right now with prisoners on it. Super Soldier prisoners."

Amari narrowed his eyes. "Why are they bringing them here?"

"Well, they're really not sure where to bring them. Sterling is actually captaining the ship. He reached out last night, and I thought... Well I thought here was the right place."

My oldest husband indicated nothing. He was good at that. Amari might have taken some time off to get me through the last months but he hadn't disappeared into happiness. The rough, negotiator was still right there. "Why would you think that?"

"Two reasons." Melissa held her ground. "First was that this is Earth. They're human beings who have never been allowed to be humans. Part of me, the sentimental part, thinks they need to come home and be here, not fighting here, but living here. Drink the water, feel the heat of our sun."

Amari shook his head. "We're not falling into that trap. Just because you bring up the water doesn't mean that we are suddenly going to feel we want to help captive Super Soldiers who once fought us in battle and let them live under our protection. Let them drink the water someplace else."

She sighed. "Okay, that was low of me. I had to try. Truth is it's because of the Z."

"Outside of war, the Z have full time jobs. Yes, some of them are here for our protection. I doubt I could separate

Brenden from my wife, but most of them have full time careers. They are not here to guard enemies who have nowhere else to go."

Melissa cleared her throat. "I don't mean to guard them. I mean to train them."

"What?" He crossed his arms over his chest. "Train them to do what?"

"To be human. To be... something. I don't know. You train men. It's what you do. I watched it for months. The Z are an incredible unit of people who are loyal, smart, and capable. Things can go wrong. They obviously did with Amber when your mother was living. But this crew is strong. I want you to give them the chance to be those men."

Katie made a happy shrieking noise, and I crossed over to her, to hand her another toy while I kept my attention on this exchange. I'd never known before I had the girls how well I could multitask with my attention.

"You want me to give our enemies the same training I give the Z? So they can be stronger when they attack us?"

"Amari, can I speak to you alone?" I wouldn't disagree with him in front of Melissa. In front of her, I was on his side, always. To me, that was loyalty.

He nodded. "Sure. Come." He extended his hand to me, and I rose, taking it. "Shane, watch the girls a second."

Shane grinned. "Watch my daughters?" He kissed Josie's head. "I love doing that."

"It is pretty great being a dad, isn't it?" Dane asked Shane as I left the room with Amari.

In the kitchen, I turned on the water. They didn't need to hear us. "They fought for Evander because Evander is their home. They've had nothing else. People fight for their homes. It's like... Mommy and Daddy telling you to go to war. They did that."

"Not all of them. If Blaze wants to move here, he can. They picked the right side."

I had to make him understand. "This isn't about right or wrong. They picked their right, it was our wrong, but they did as they were raised and born to do. Amari, they need another home. We need for them to pick us next time. There'll be a next time. Maybe not in our lifetime, and hopefully not in the girls'. But maybe their sons or daughters. There is always a next time. Don't you want the descendants of those men to fight for us?"

"What makes you think I can rehab them? I'm not in any way trained for this."

I pulled him to me. "Because you're you. Because success is what you do. Find a way to help them and make it profitable."

He pressed his forehead to mine. "I'll try."

"Good." I grinned at him.

"I know you just partially manipulated me. You're better at it than Melissa."

I shook my hand. "No, you just want to fuck me so it seems that way."

He threw his head back, laughing. "That is absolutely true."

Amari let go of me. "I'm getting rid of them so we can do just that. Come say goodbye."

I turned off the water and followed him to the front room.

"I'm going to do it. I'll rehab who can be rehabbed and if they can't then I'm sticking them on a ship headed straight to the Dark Planets. They can go find a life for themselves there. But yes, I'll try. Don't be surprised when they start showing up on Mars Station ready to work for you. That'll be my first suggestion of work."

Melissa grinned. "Sounds good, Amari. Nolan loves a good security team."

———

I'd thought that winter was gone, but it turned out it had only gone on hiatus for a few days. The afternoon Melissa and her crew left us, the Super Soldiers arrived, landing in the midst of a blizzard. It marked new days for all of us. Hunter took a trip to go look at the new security blasters being installed on the North Pole of the planet, and I'd officially left the girls in the hands of two nannies and their two guards, who I finally decided I trusted.

Shane had promised to get home to them before dinner, which meant they'd only be alone for three hours without any one of us checking on them.

Amari wanted me with him to quote "look at what kind of mess I'd convinced him to get into."

Sterling stepped off the ship. He nodded at Amari. "Really nice to see you up, brother."

Amari grinned at him. "Well, I needed a good nap."

"Heard you broke the med machine. How'd you do that?" He scratched his head. "Knocks me on my ass."

Everyone asked Amari this now. I was pretty sure he hated it. "I really don't remember it. I guess I just really wanted to see Amber before she gave birth."

This made Sterling turn his attention to me. "Diana asked me to see the girls while I'm here. Is that okay?"

"Sure. Tell her I miss her."

"Will do." He cleared his throat. "I'm bringing you a mess."

"I fix messes. It's what I do." Amari could feign confidence with the best of the them.

Hours later, I wasn't so sure I'd done the right thing convincing Amari to do this. Fifteen of the angriest people I'd ever seen disembarked from that shuttle. Amari had placed them under guard in the top floor of the orphanage we'd built. There were only a few children there so far as we were working on relocating the kids to places where their extended families were. Only after it was clear they had no one did they come to live there.

I wasn't sure it was a good idea to put them in the same building with the Super Soldiers, but Amari seemed to be certain about it. He wanted to see. That was all he said. In the meantime his best Z were watching them.

When I asked what he wanted to see, he didn't answer me. This was Z land, and much as I'd temporarily led them, I wasn't one of them, and I didn't want to be.

The men wouldn't even tell us their names. Right now they were numbers, and I hated it.

I slumped down on the couch next to a sleeping Shane, both girls sprawled out on his chest. The nannies had been gone when I got here. Did that mean he didn't like what he saw when he arrived or he'd just told them to go home? I touched his cheek, running my finger off the slight scruff there.

His eyes fluttered open. "Hey, beautiful. Guess we decided to take a nap."

"I'll never know how you can sleep with them on you. I'm always terrified they're going to get hurt."

He shook his head. "They're safe with me."

"Yes, Master Chen." I rolled my eyes. "Where did the nannies go?"

"They were great. Girls were fine. When I got home, I

simply decided I preferred it to just be us when we're home, and I sent them off. They'll be back tomorrow morning. How was it being back in the real world outside of this haven you had built for us?"

I thought about that. "Nice to be dressed, to be around adults. Horrible in some ways. Those men... they're not Sterling or Canyon or Rohan. They're not even Blaze and his guys. These men are rough and hurt. I don't know if we can help them."

Shane adored me with his gaze. "We can. You were right to push Amari on it. Some of them will get better with time. Some of them will need a push. He can do it."

I hoped he was right.

SHANE

I walked to the water. With late freezes, sometimes the water could get bacteria in it. I had Katie on my shoulder. She was bundled up in a jacket one of the older women had given us. Two Z trailed behind us, but they were giving us space.

I'd take Josie here, too, when she wasn't fussing. Amber thought she was cutting teeth, and I didn't want to wake her since she slept. But Katie was awake so Lady Katherine got to come.

I still couldn't believe I'd made two female babies. Her mother's violet eyes stared up at me, and I grinned. Yes, they were Amber's, but they had an edge no one commented on, but I was sure my brothers could also see. Those were Chen eyes. Her mother wouldn't hurt anyone; she was a healer, unless she felt they threatened those she loved. This child would be ruthless, and we'd have to temper it.

The Z training helped do just that.

We reached the water, and I stopped, taking a breath. It was healthy. The freeze hadn't disrupted that. I put my hand in it, feeling the cool wetness on my fingers. Katie stared, wide eyed, and watched.

"Your turn." I placed her chubby fingers in the water, and she gasped. "Do you feel it?"

She stuck her fist in her mouth, and for a second I could feel it, her energy, so familiar there was no question she was ours, mine and Amber's.

"You do feel it. That's your birthright. Yours and Josie's. Uncle Amari says you guys are the heirs even if he has children someday, because you were born first, and he loves you like you're his. He's declared it so it's so. Oh, and Katherine, I've got bad news, Josie's going to have more choices than you. You'll have to run Chen. I'm sorry about that and also not sorry. But, Katie, this water? This is pretty much what we do. The Chens have protected the waters of Earth since the bombs went off. You'll never know those bombs. I'm going to see to that."

AMBER

AMARI POINTED at the scene in front of him. "That's what I was looking for."

I leaned on his arm. Three of the fifteen Super Soldiers were sitting on benches outside of the orphanage, playing with the kids. I wasn't really sure what to think or what to make of it. "Are they okay? Is it safe?"

"Those three are. They'll start training immediately. Anyone who could live in a house with orphans and not end up playing with them is suspect. They're all essentially orphans themselves. The other test would be to let loose a rumor I plan to train those orphans to do unspeakable things and see if they object. I don't, obviously. That being said, I might wake up dead with this crew so we're not going to do that."

I shook my head. "They can hear us talking about them. Even from this distance."

"I'm well aware." He kissed me. "Go home. It's going to be a late night for me. I'm going to miss my girls."

I'd never been more glad to not have his job than right then. How did he know what to do with people?

Waverly approached us quietly. "Hey, you two."

"Hi there." I loved seeing her, but my joy quickly fell. She had tears in her eyes. "You're here to say goodbye, too."

"It's been really good having you here, Waverly." Amari stepped away, nodding at me. He was giving me a minute.

I embraced her tightly. "You're going to be so missed. Are you heading back to The Farm?"

"We think that's where we can be of the most use and we're going to go see if there is anything left of our house. Ari wanted to wait here until he was sure you were all okay."

It would have been weird to hug her again, too needy, too much, so I didn't. "I couldn't have done any of this without him. And your husbands saved us, well your future husbands, the version of them in the future." I never did know how to talk about time travel. "And Canyon is why I'm here to begin with. Maybe why any of us are, since we'd never have worked with my husbands on the war effort if they weren't with me. And... that's all because of you. Canyon wouldn't have known how to do that if he didn't love you. So really, Waverly, you saved all of us."

She laughed, throwing her head back. "That's ridiculous. And wonderful. I love you, Amber. It won't be the same on that cold planet without you. Come and visit, a lot, please. After we kick Evander back through the black hole. Just two ships. I keep asking myself, how much trouble could two Evander ships make?"

Waverly and I both knew the answer to that. "Be safe out there."

"I will." She kissed my cheek. "Be safe here on this blue planet. Don't let them get lost, okay? They were without you. Now, they seem so centered, so in love. What happened to the Shane that called that first day to find out why someone hacked the tablet? He's nowhere to be found. This Shane—he's different."

I had to agree with her. Shane was the most overtly different. He was the one who showed it on the outside. But there were large changes in Hunter and Amari too. No, that was wrong. They'd always been these people. We'd simply never known each other.

"I won't let them get lost." That was a promise from me as much to me as to her.

Her smile was huge. "Oh, here, comes Ari."

I spun around. I really hated goodbyes. He walked up, putting his arm around Waverly's waist. "Well, it's time for us to go. We can physically not restrain Jackson any further. He might take apart your entire development and rebuild it if we don't let the pirate get back into space."

I could actually see that happening. "You know I couldn't have done this, all of those months alone, and then the ones when I didn't know if they'd live or die, without you. You've been my mentor and my friend. When you go back to tell me not to wake Sienna, not to tell my husbands that I have her, tell me in front of them that they'd move mountains for me. It's a Z thing."

His smile was fast. "Amari already gave me the full code. It's more than the mountains. It's the water, too. You're my friend, too, Amber. Get back to work when you are up to it. You're a very good doctor. I'd let you operate on my kids, on Waverly."

That was a huge compliment, and I took it as such. "Thank you, Ari. Soon, I think. I've left the house twice in two days. That's pretty huge. See you sometime on the other side of the galaxy."

He pointed at me. "When we are finally finished with Evander."

"When Sienna is safe. Since that somehow plays a role. Hey, the next time you tell me that we'll both be in our current timeline. We'll know why that mattered."

He nodded. "See you soon."

I hoped we did.

━━━

I walked past the orphanage. The same three Super Soldiers were outside, this time talking to Kelton, and there were two more on the ground with the kids. That made five of fifteen. Was it possible to remake men like this? Put them with children, quiet conversations. I guessed when I'd been thinking of Amari doing this I'd thought of him doing some sort of Z mind thing and getting them to think about energy.

He was just leaving them be, as far as I could tell. Maybe it was just for now.

One of them broke away from the group and ran over to me. "Hey, you."

I stopped short. Was he talking to me? "Yes?"

Kelton chased after him. "This is Dr. Chen. She's married to the Chens. They're in charge here, as you know. Address her that way, not as hey, you. What do you want with her?"

The soldier took a long breath. He was tall, broad shouldered like all of them were. His hair was long, to his shoulders, and a long scar marred the side of his face. "You have babies."

I swallowed. "I do."

"Their father. I can hear how he's connected to them.

We resonate interesting sounds. It confuses you people. But it's true."

Kelton glared at him. "If you have something to say about this get to it otherwise let's let Dr. Chen get on her way."

"Master Kelton." I put my hand on his arm. I noticed we were not doing without titles right now. "This man is speaking to me. It's okay. I don't need to rush him. What's your name?"

He frowned. "They call me Devil."

Well, that was unusual but Diana's husband was named Sterling so who knew where they'd come up with this stuff. "How can I help you, Devil? You were asking about the babies and my husband Shane?"

"Shane, okay." He fiddled with his fingers, circling them, one around the other. "His heart isn't okay. I can hear it from here. It's beating irregularly."

My body went cold. "Okay. Kelton, get Ari from the comm. Don't let him leave. I need him here. I'm going to Shane, now."

Where was he? I had to think about it. He was at the water today. He was going to go test it and then take it back to the labs before he started a schedule again for all of the local waters. I rushed, calling into my earpiece. Brenden wasn't with me. We'd had him back off just a little bit when I was what Amari called on property. There were always Z around. I didn't need a tail. Brenden was still in charge when it came to my safety if I went somewhere.

Lately, he must have been bored. "Brenden, I need Shane. There's something wrong with his heart. Don't panic him. Please. But get someone to him. Sit him down. A Super Soldier can hear it."

I rounded the corner toward the water just as two Z

made my husband sit down. Shane looked up as I came in. "Amber, what the fuck?"

"Shane, not to worry. We're going to check out your heart."

He put his hand on my chest. "Thought that was over."

So had I. "Feel okay?"

"I'm a little bit tired, but the girls were up last night. You were, too. I'm otherwise fine."

I kissed him, hard. Where was Ari?

Brenden ran up behind me. "Too late to stop Ari. They're gone."

Then it was me. I didn't know any of the doctors moving in here who I'd be working with. They weren't even due to start until tomorrow. This hadn't been well done. Too many moving pieces, and none of us paying close enough attention to it.

"Come with me," I took his hand. "It's all going to be fine."

Looked like I was back to work today, and with one of the five most important people in the universe counting on me to keep him safe.

———

I stared at the scanner as Shane stared at me in the med bay.

"I feel fine, and I don't want to get back in that thing." He chewed on his fingernail.

I ran the scan again. No damage from the drug. That was what it kept showing, over and over.

"Amber? I feel fine."

I knew he did, but his EKG had been wrong. Now, it was fine. There was obvious damage. Unless there wasn't.

I turned around to the Z waiting by the door. "I need

one of you who was here when Master Shane was a baby. An older Z. Now. Please."

He didn't question me, running out the door.

"Amber," Shane said again. "Look at me. Not the scanner."

I did as he asked. "Shane, I'm glad you feel fine. I am enormously glad. But something is wrong. Let me do this. Think about something other than how irritated you are that you're in here. You know, it's my birthday coming up. Think about what we should do to celebrate."

He brightened at that. "I know it is. We've already discussed it, the guys and me. We have something planned. I'm not telling you what."

Let him think about that. "Is it related to water?"

"You know, despite all evidence to the contrary, I'm not obsessed with water."

I grinned at him while I also looked at the scanner. "It is, isn't it? It's water."

The Z I'd sent out arrived with an older Zansi Warrior and Amari in tow. My oldest husband stood over my left shoulder as Hunter ran through the door.

"Talk to me," Amari whispered.

"In a second." Right this second I needed the older man. "Sir, my name is Amber. I don't think we've met."

He nodded, once. "Yes, Dr. Chen. I've been with the family a long time. I served their late father and was on the ships fighting Evander with Master Hunter during the war."

"Did you know Master Shane when he was a baby?" I needed someone who had. My hunch was right. I knew it was. Ari had taught me to trust it. Dane hadn't missed this. He simply hadn't known what to look for.

"I did, indeed. I've always known the Masters Chen. Since they were each born."

"Amber?" Shane said to me again, and I took his hand in mine.

They had to let me get through this or I was going to kick them all out of the room and sedate Shane. "Was he a fussy baby?"

"Oh, yes, out of all three of them, he was. He cried all of the time."

"Well, now we at least know where Katie got it from." Shane sighed. "Can I go now?"

It registered on Hunter's face, and the second it did, he strode over. "His heart wasn't injured in the Evander incident. No, it was always off. Since birth. We were so rarely scanned. Father didn't want people to know how the Chen do what we do. If they can find it in our DNA they can copy it. That was the idea, to protect us. We grew."

Amari nodded. "We were healthy. The energy came to us. There was no need."

"Hunter got hurt. Dad stood over the med machine the whole time. They kept him awake."

I remembered that story, vividly. Hunter talked about how his uncle talked him out of panic. I hadn't understood why he was awake.

I pointed at all three of them. "Sit down. All of you. We're scanning for birth conditions. Things we wouldn't look at now. You're grown-ups. You should be dead if it's some of this stuff. But you're Chens. You move energy. I'm not ruling anything out. All three of you. Now."

Hunter hopped up on the table fast. Amari did it slower. In the end, they all stopped complaining. I found what I was looking for, and I wasn't even surprised by the results.

Amari and Hunter were fine. Shane had been born with a birth defect that should have killed him before the age of two. A small clot, hidden from view unless we looked for it, in the left ventricle of his heart. In the old days they'd have called it a widow maker. After the bombs, when whatever was left in the atmosphere here on Earth happened, things that used to happen to old people started showing up in children. It was a two-generation problem. Those with these issues hadn't lived to reproduce.

Shane should have died in childhood.

The good news was the machine would get it out. Now that I'd found it. These things were miracle workers, but it took us to run them, to know what they missed.

"Amari, go get the girls, please."

I already knew what I'd find.

━━━

The machine fixed Shane in half an hour and Katie in ten minutes. Josie was free of the issue.

"Would it have eventually killed him?" Amari passed me a glass of wine. This was the old kind from the third vintage after the bombs in quadrant two. We sat on our porch and stared at the night together. One of the new doctors arrived early and was eager to start, so I'd put him in charge.

I pointed to my breasts. "I can't drink. Not yet. Soon." I might wean the girls onto synthetic breast milk soon. I'd had to pump to leave them the last two days, and I really hated it. The synthetic stuff wasn't quite as good for them. I sighed. Nope, I'd keep doing it. I loved those girls. I'd make this work.

Amari set down his glass. "Sorry, love."

"I didn't say you couldn't drink it. Don't want to waste it now that you opened a bottle and poured."

He nodded. "Fair enough. Would it have killed him? Katie?"

"Yes, probably. And her, too. Maybe early. I don't know if she'd have made it like he did. I think she was trying to tell me. I think he tried to tell your mother and father. The cranky. Doesn't have to mean anything is wrong, but I think it did. Then they get older and give up." I put my head between my knees.

"Is that your medical opinion, doctor, or a tired mom and wife who had a scare?"

I kicked him not lightly in the shin, and he oomphed. "Sorry. Shouldn't have done that. They were both cranky babies."

"And I have brown eyes and so does Brenden. You know better than most. Correlation does not causation make. Go see your daughter. Go check on your husband."

I kissed his cheek. "One of the Super Soldiers saved them."

"I know. It might be... good... to have them here."

It might be.

———

Hunter snored lightly, Katie slept next to him on one side, in her little basket Shane had made her so she could safely co-sleep with us. Josie was on his other side, in her basket. They'd taken to sleeping in their cribs, but tonight, I guessed Hunter wanted them close. He had his hand on Katie's back as though he wanted to feel her breathe in her sleep. I walked over and did the same. Her breaths were good, and her pulse was strong. She needed to rest after her ordeal, but she'd be fine.

Her heart was healthy now.

The girls were thriving. We'd caught this. By the universe, today we were lucky.

Hunter was beautiful when he slept. He'd hate that description, only it applied. I left him to go check on Shane.

He was face down on his bed, snoring louder than Hunter had been. And they all teased me about my snoring. I shook my head.

Before I could overthink it, I crawled on top of him, which woke him immediately.

He rolled over, keeping me on top of him the whole time. "This is a nice wake up."

I kissed him. I didn't want to talk. I just wanted to feel him. I was glad for stolen moments. I was stealing this one.

He kissed me back, not saying a word. Maybe he understood. Some things were just too much to be said. Every time we were together, every time we'd done anything, he'd been at risk of dying. I put my hand over his heart and felt it beat. He wrapped his arms around me, holding onto me tight as he kissed me.

I bit down on his lip, and he grinned.

I leaned back, pulling on his shirt. Once it was off, I started at his neck and kissed downward, everywhere I could reach on his chest.

He let me for a while until he took off my shirt. Then his hands were everywhere. I didn't stop what I was doing. He could touch me, but damn it, I was going to kiss him everywhere. That was all I wanted.

He pulled off my pants and it gave me no choice but to stop my constant kissing of his chest. Shane pushed me down on the bed beneath him. We were both naked, and he was so hard that he poked into me, brushing my leg with his length.

I stroked him once.

"Shit." He flared his nostrils. "Amber. I love you."

I sent him all of my love, hoping he'd feel it, and he did. Shane closed his eyes for a second, and when he opened them, his dark depths bore into me like he'd taken control of my soul for a second. "You love me that much, Amber?"

"I do." I had to say something, and I found my voice. "And I will not lose you."

He kissed my neck. "You won't. Ever."

I wrapped my legs around him, drawing him near until he entered me. This was what I needed. Him. In me.

"Ride me hard. So hard. You can't break me. I need it."

He drew me toward him until I was on my elbows. "If that's what you want, then that's what I want."

Shane listened. He fucked me until I couldn't think, until the day was behind me, until I was sure this was all not about to blow up in my face and I would be alone again. He fucked and fucked me because that was what I needed and he loved me that much.

And then finally, we came together. I dug my fingers into his back, probably hard enough to draw blood, but he never let go of me, never objected. Shane loved me. I adored him. And his heart was safe and secure.

I was going to keep it that way.

I lay across his body, neither of us sleeping. Footsteps in the hall caught my attention, and I recognized them as Amari. He had the surest gate of all of my husbands. They stopped when he must have gone into Hunter's room with the girls.

"Come with me." I drew Shane up, and he didn't question me.

We dressed quickly, in as much as we needed to sleep, and walked quietly into the bedroom. Hunter still snored, his hand on Katie's back. He hadn't moved. Amari looked up; he was on the left side of the bed next to Josie.

I touched his hand, and he squeezed it.

Hunter's eyes flew open. He sat up, slowly, not disturbing the babies. For a moment, the three of us didn't move. Then Hunter nodded toward the floor. His brothers rose, and I followed suit. They sat, and Amari patted the floor next to him. I joined him down there, realization hitting me. They wanted to meditate. We were all together. It was time.

"I'm still not as good at this as you guys are."

Shane grinned at me. "You threw your consciousness through space. I think you're plenty good at this."

Okay, that was true.

Amari took my hand in his, and Shane took the other one. I met Hunter's gaze, and he winked at me. I doubted very much the three of them held hands when they did this, considering that they weren't holding Hunter's hand.

Amari grinned. "This makes up for standing me up outside on the porch."

I nudged him. "I got distracted, and then I heard you come inside."

He still smiled. "I'm not upset. This is perfect."

I closed my eyes, and we all seemed to breathe together. I concentrated on my hands, on my legs, on how my stomach felt. I really was much better at this than I'd been when I'd first tried it. I didn't need direction to know when to take my thoughts outside my body to the universe. I thought about my girls. They really were doing so much better, and discovering Katie's heart issue meant that was never going to cause her problems. I could almost sense their sleeping energy. Josie's quieter, easier personality. Katie's ability to control the feelings of everyone in the room with either her charm or her anger. In some ways, they were very similar to Paloma and me. I'd never given that any thought before. As much as they were Chens, and it was hard for me to see otherwise, they were mine as well.

There were parts of their life that would be dictated by the fact that I was their mother.

I moved on. There were problems in the universe. Evander wasn't gone. I wanted to help, and I also didn't want to leave, didn't want my people to leave. I couldn't fix this by myself. I couldn't make Evander go back through the black hole and never return. I was one person and I didn't have those answers.

Still, I concentrated until I felt my consciousness naturally drift back to the here and now.

It must have hit all of us at the same time. My guys all opened their beautiful, dark eyes. My own vision adjusted to the darkness while I meditated and now it was like I could see as easily as I did during the day.

Amari kissed my cheek before he rose and returned to the bed. Hunter placed his kiss on my lips but got back next to Katie where he'd been. Shane squeezed my hand before he placed a small kiss on the spot where my neck met my shoulder. I shuddered. I loved how these men loved me, and I hoped they could feel how much that was returned.

Shane lay down on the other side of Katie. These beds were huge, and I was grateful for it. I climbed through the middle, onto Hunter, and then slid to his side so I was between him and Josie. Hunter rolled slightly, his other arm going across my stomach and holding on. It didn't take long before they were all settled down. Hunter's deep breathing turned to light snores in no time, and the shift of energy in the room told me they were all out cold. How could they sleep when so much energy still buzzed through my veins?

I closed my eyes and just breathed. This was my family. We were all safe, we were all in this bed. Everyone would be okay until the morning.

I just listened to them. The slow, strong breath that was Amari. Hunter's light snores. The way that Shane sighed in his sleep. The girls made sweet baby noises.

My family was everything to me.

I'd almost lost it so many times.

The girls I should never had have if not for Hunter's genius being transformed into a medical miracle. If I touched my lower abdomen, I could almost feel the device implanted inside of me. It was a small, hard box. It was amazing. Not quite nanotech but close.

Funny how one day back at it and my mind turned back to medicine. Like a light switch going on, I thought of Sienna. She was dying somewhere in the galaxy, in a med machine that wouldn't heal her unless we came up with a cure for the G strand of flu. That wasn't happening anytime soon. Cash had cured Flu F, once. One strand of it. But he'd had nothing but time and no wars to content with. If we stuck him in a room, which Diana would never allow, and let him do nothing else, he might have an answer in ten years.

But there were immune enhancers. Evander did that to the Super Soldiers. It was why they didn't get sick. Could we... nano that? Like the way Ari had healed Canyon's eyes?

I sat forward. Immune enhancement in a nano tech that was put in a box like mine that was forever feeding nanos into her body and suppressing the illness until it could be cured. I chewed on my bottom lip.

Wade would need nanos. He could tap into a Super Soldier's immune system. He had four of them there with him, and I could upload the schematic of what was inside of me. The problem was the nanos.

He was going to have to get to The Farm and get some from Canyon's eyes.

We could save Sienna long enough that they could wake her up and find out why the hell Evander wanted her.

Was I crazy? Could it work? No, I was smart. I was capable. I'd been trained by the best minds in the universe.

I stared at my daughters. By the universe, they would grow up to be confident, to be sure of themselves. Well, of course they would. They were Chen daughters and the Chens were never short of confidence. It was one of the things I loved about them so fucking much.

This was why Ari had said I had to wait to wake her. He knew in the future that I would have an epiphany. An a-ha moment. This was it.

I hated time travel but right at this moment I loved it. So fucking hard. I had clarity. There was something that only I could do for the universe.

My sister stood at the door, holding a pot of something she set down in my kitchen before she whirled around, her hands on her hips. "Where are the girls?"

"They're sleeping. It's very early." I hadn't even had any coffee yet. My husbands were up, but I wasn't used to seeing Paloma this early. In fact, I hadn't seen her very much at all lately. "You're coming to tell me you're leaving."

She shook her head. "What? No. Just the opposite, actually."

My sister prepared me coffee. I watched her, my brain trying to catch up to this moment. "What does that mean?"

"Tommy is going to speak to Amari about this today." She handed me the coffee. "Drink that. It's good."

I sipped. She was right. It was heaven. How was it that my sister could make the same coffee I made every morning and it tasted so good when she did it and like sludge when I did? I shook my head. She was gifted in the kitchen. Everything she touched was perfection. I needed to stay away from the room all together.

"It's wonderful. What is he going to talk to him about?"

She grinned at me, a piece of her long brown hair falling over her shoulder. Applesauce jumped up on the counter, rubbing against her. She petted him for a second before coming to me. We were seeing the cat more and more since the crying stopped.

Paloma finally answered me. "He is going to talk about us staying here on Earth. Amari put a call out for businesses. We traveled around Chen Empire looking for spots. I didn't want to get your hopes up in case they changed their minds. But we've all found spots that would work for us. So assuming Amari would be okay with having the Sandlers here, we want to stay."

I threw my arms around her. I didn't even know I was going to do that, but I did because my sister was staying. "Evander is still out there, and you're going to stay."

She squeezed me. "Evander is still out there, and we're going to stay. Help secure Earth, maybe, with what Tommy is going to do. He's going to build ships. Here. They'll be available for defense."

I stared at her. "I... I can't speak for Amari. I don't know what he's going to say."

"We'll work out the details." Amari walked in. Paloma poured him coffee. He was really never going to want mine again. "I'm never going to tell my brothers-in-law they can't stay on Earth. I don't own Earth. As for Chen Empire, yes they can build here. It's a great idea. Clay's going to practice law. Keith will teach. What about Quinn?"

She sighed. "That's where it gets complicated. He wants to open a casino."

Amari blinked. "On the edge I bet. Of the Empire. We'll make it a vacation destination."

Her mouth fell open. "That's what he wanted."

"Great. I'll meet with them this morning. Good coffee." He bent over to kiss my cheek. "But I like the horrible stuff your sister concocts. She's going to save the whole universe. Did she tell you she figured out how to save Sienna and possibly revolutionize the treatment of the flu forever? At three in the morning?"

Paloma stared at me. "No. She never tells me anything like that. She just does amazing things quietly and moves on with her life as though she didn't do anything substantial at all. Come on, Amber, brag."

I might have been incapable of it. "Are you going to open a restaurant?"

She clapped her hands together. "I am."

This was the best morning. It really was. If only there weren't two Evander ships still out there in the universe, plowing through the Dark Planets, that we couldn't do anything about, couldn't see, couldn't find.

Cold wafted over me, making goosebumps run over my arms. "That is awesome, Paloma. I'm... I'm having a hard time with the idea that you want to stay here? Not The Farm with Diana?"

"A Farm on a remote part of the universe was Diana's idea. Not mine. It was... refuge but not how I want to spend life. Even with Evander out there, in the Dark Planets, and Diana getting ready to launch another fleet after them, I want to make plans for my children, how we're going to live." She smiled at me. "You're my sister. Unless you don't want me here, Amber, I thought maybe we could do a restart on The Delacroix family together. Raise our babies differently, together."

I loved that idea. Still, I had to say. "You know we're not

done. I can't see it. When the reckoning comes in the Dark Planets, I just have this feeling, we're all going to be there."

She nodded. "I have the same feeling and... this is going to sound weird."

Whatever she was going to say couldn't have been any weirder than hearing Sienna in my head. "Tell me."

"I feel like it was always going to come down to the Dark Planets—that place that even those who live there feel like they don't know. I've never been there. It's... it's exactly where they would hide and maybe we should have always known that."

I took another sip of my coffee. "I've been there. I was shot there. And I'll be honest, I'm worried. I don't know if Artemis got my message about Sienna. I don't know if Trenton can pilot her around those unknown places, or if even the Super Soldiers on that ship will know what to do out there."

She took my hand. "Oh come on, Amber. It's Artemis. She's got this." Paloma covered her mouth. "I'm talking about the ship like she's living. Sorry. Maybe I'm super tired. Aaron is teething again. Where are the girls? Wake them up already."

I set down my coffee. If it was possible to survive what was happening out there in the Dark Planets, Artemis was the ship to do it with. C.J. had taken Malice with him. Two ships from the other side of the galaxy. So far from home. Helping us try to set things right.

"I'll get the girls."

———

Six months later...

. . .

"I can't believe this is happening." My sister wore her Sandler red, looking stunning, like something out of fiction, not real life. I'd put myself together as best I could, but it had been so long since I'd dressed up I'd hardly remembered how to do it.

Shane liked me in black so that was what I'd donned, with purple touches to speak of the Z. Paloma and I stared at each other.

"Why are we doing this again?"

"Evander wanted a meeting. They're getting one." I hated this as much as she did and the pomp Amari pulled out to greet them. It was all for show but still... I'd have rather stayed home for this and done just about anything else.

He wouldn't even tell me what he was going to say.

Hunter and Quinn met us by the door. Quinn took Paloma's arm, and Hunter linked his fingers with mine. He whispered in my ear. "If I could have picked anything in the world for you to wear tonight it would have been this."

"Thank you." I had too many butterflies for compliments right then. "Why are we doing this?"

"Evander wanted a meeting." He kissed my hand. "They're getting one they'll never forget."

I hadn't been in the conference hall since we'd rebuilt it. Now a separate building unto itself, it was an impressive structure. I hadn't designed it. This was all my husbands. They had specific things they'd wanted. Shane nodded at me as I entered even as he undressed me with his eyes. My nipples hardened. I never ceased to desire my men. I didn't think I ever would.

The room was crowded, filled with members of the Chen Empire and the Z, as well as the five people here on behalf of Evander. I sat down in the front, in seats designated for Paloma and me. Leaning over, I whispered to my sister. "Anything short of surrender seems nonsensical to me."

She nodded. "Look. They have a feed going." She nodded toward the monitors at the top of the room. "Who do you think Amari invited to watch?"

"When he goes tight lipped like he has over this, I get a little nervous."

She took my hand in hers. "Do you suppose these guys would be intimidated if they'd seen him last night holding Josie while she threw applesauce all over him?"

I preferred those times to these. "Do you think people would believe Tommy lets Ben ride him like a horse?"

Her smile was huge. "Probably not."

"Let's get started." Amari rose and the room fell silent. "We're here today because representatives from Evander Corporation asked for a meeting." He nodded toward them. "Gentlemen, we're here. We're listening."

The royal *we*. Hunter sat to his left with Shane on his right. The Sandlers were on the stage, too. Around the room were small waterfalls, meant to represent the Chens' relationship with water on our planet. Or at least that was what I assumed. I was pretty sure I'd been nursing and exhausted when they'd designed this.

If I'd heard the discussion, I really didn't remember.

The representative rose. He was a tall man with blond hair and brown eyes. He wore the insignia of Evander on his shirt.

"We are here today to open a dialogue with you about doing business with Evander Corporation. Our new CEO, Steven Segwick, sees opportunity for us all to make profit."

Amari tilted his head just slightly. "You people change CEOs like most people use tissues."

Everyone in the room laughed, everyone but me. Amari wasn't funny. He didn't make jokes. This was deadly serious to him.

The representative nodded. "There has been a lot of upheaval lately, but the board is solidified."

"I see. And now you want to do business with the Chen Empire? That's what you're saying to me?"

My body tingled with alertness. Amari didn't ask people questions in public he didn't already know the answers to. What was he doing?

"Yes." The man bowed again. It was an affect, not at all the same as the way the Z bowed to each other, almost like someone had told him the Chens walked around bowing the whole time.

Amari rose slowly. "I might be interested in doing business with you except for a few... small... problems."

The man approached Amari, talking fast. "Perhaps we can negotiate through those issues."

"Maybe we can." Amari nodded. "You tell me how we can work through how you destroyed Oceania, killing thousands upon thousands of people, my wife almost one of them."

People around me shifted in their seats, but I stayed unmoving, my face passive. This was about to go very badly for the representative from Evander.

"That was an unfortunate decision by one of the previous CEOs. Your wife sits here, I believe. Unharmed."

Paloma shook her head. "Wrong response."

"She does. Yes. Then you attacked Earth, went to war with us, killed hundreds of people, took my brothers and me hostage, and injected drugs meant to kill us into our bloodstream. You are still here on this side of the galaxy after repeatedly being told to leave, and are currently after a woman who has done nothing to you. I am sick to death of all the phony changing of CEOs as an excuse for what you people do." Amari pointed to him. "No, we can't negotiate. No, we can't do business or come to terms. Ever."

Hunter was a blur of movement as he held the representative by his throat. A second later he held the man's head under water in one of the small waterfall features in the room. Everyone was silent. This was not the first time I'd seen Hunter kill someone. It wouldn't be the last. It was never Amari, although he always sanctioned it, and it was never Shane, although he could have done it, too. This was Hunter's role because he'd made it his role.

I rose and walked slowly to him. Amari was done. He'd turned his back on the rest of the representatives who now shook in their seats. I glanced at them. "Run away. Run fast. Go back through the black hole. Tell your CEOs and your board they are not welcome here on this side of the galaxy. If you continue to force us to chase you through the Dark Planets, you will wish you'd never been born. Unless the rest of you want to drown in our waters, then you need to run away. Now."

They listened to me. The four remaining men fled the room faster than I would have thought they could. Hunter stepped away from the now drowned man. His gaze found my own, and I put my hand out for him to take it. Let whoever watched us on that feed see we were united, that we were one family, that we were not playing games.

"Any member of the Evander Corporation who steps foot on Earth to do anything but surrender will find themselves drowned in our waters." It was Shane who spoke.

These were my husbands. They were brutal. They were rough. They had no mercy for their enemies. They could bend air and energy. They defeated their enemies and survived assaults thrown at them from every direction.

They held the loyalty of thousands of men who counted on them for their safety and their futures.

And I loved them. Beyond reason, beyond war, beyond sense. I was Amber Chen. Earth was closed to Evander.

Dearest Reader,

Thank you so much for reading Rising Tides (Wings of Artemis #10) and taking this journey through space with me. There are two more novels to come before the completion of the series and I am hard at work to get those to you just as quickly as I can type. If you are interested, please come by and join my readers' group on Facebook where you can be the first to hear book news from me and interact with other people who enjoy my books. Find us here: http://www.facebook.com/groups/rebeccasrandomness

While you wait for the next book, you might like to read my completed five book series Last Hope, that is a paranormal reverse harem romance, you can find the first book, Tradition Be Damned, right here: https://amzn.to/2EmE9OR

If you have a minute and could leave this book a review, I'd be so grateful. Reviews help authors get their books in front of readers.

Please turn the page to see a list of my 80+ books that I've written in my ten-year career and to learn more about me.

Thanks so much for reading,
    RR

Please Turn the page for a complete list of my books

ABOUT THE AUTHOR

As a teenager, I would hide in my room to read my favorite romance novels when I was supposed to be doing my homework.

I am the mother of three adorable boys and I am fortunate to be married to my best friend. I live in Austin Texas where I am determined to eat all the barbecue in town.

I am in love with science fiction, fantasy, and the paranormal and try to use all of these elements in my writing. I've been told I'm a little bloodthirsty so I hope that when you read my work you'll enjoy the action packed ride that always ends in romance. I love to write series because I love to see characters develop over time and it always makes me happy to see my favorite characters make guest appearances in other books.

In my world anything is possible, anything can happen, and you should suspect that it will.

I'd love to hear from you! Please visit my website at www.rebeccaroyce.com to sign up for my newsletter and learn about my books!

Here's where you can find me online:

www.rebeccaroyce.com

Rebecca's Randomness Reading Group https://www.facebook.com/groups/RebeccasRandomness/

https://www.facebook.com/authorrebeccaroyce/

www.twitter.com/rebeccaroyce

Instagram: rebeccaroyce79
MeWe: RebeccaRoyce
Cheers!!
Rebecca

OTHER BOOKS BY REBECCA ROYCE...

Wings of Artemis

Kidnapped By Her Husbands https://amzn.to/2BQdUxy

Rescued by Their Wife https://amzn.to/2Rr9as4

Crashing Into Destiny https://amzn.to/2VkyXRL

Meeting Them https://amzn.to/2BLPaXm

Reclaiming Their Love https://amzn.to/2GKAw8E

Loving Them https://amzn.to/2BKDmEK

Ship Called Malice https://amzn.to/2BNputj

Saving Them https://amzn.to/2SsrBtH

Dark Demise https://amzn.to/2VidXv3

Light Unfolding https://amzn.to/2GO6Yqr

Still Waters https://amzn.to/2CFePT8

Rising Tides https://amzn.to/2MCdTlM

Lost Star (coming soon)

Pointed Arrow (coming soon)

Last Hope (completed series)

Tradition Be Damned

Past Be Damned

Destiny Be Damned

Compassion Be Damned

Future Be Damned

Dragon Wars (completed series)

Forever

Eternal

Always

Evermore

Endless

Wards and Wands

Hexed and Vexed

Curse Reversed

Meow, Baby (novella in the Petting Them antho written with Ripley Proserpina)

Tragic Magic (Coming Soon)

Safe Haven

Everywhere and Nowhere

Dimension X (coming soon)

More coming soon....

Soul Bound

Prisoner of the Dragons

More coming soon....

Shadow Promised

Strange Days

Weird Nights

Bizarre Years

More coming soon...

The Warrior (completed series)

Initiation

Driven

Subversive

Redemption

Justice

Warrior World (spin off of The Warrior, completed series)

Deacon

Micah

Jason

The Westervelt Wolves (completed series)

Her Wolf

Summer's Wolf

Wolf Reborn

Wolf's Valentine

Wolf's Magic

Alpha Wolf

Angel's Wolf

Darkest Wolf

Lone Wolf

Fallen Alpha

Alpha Rising

Alpha's Strength

Alpha's Sacrifice

Alpha's Truth

Alpha Enticing

Hidden Alpha (coming soon)

The Capes (completed series)

Seductive Powers

Adrenaline Rush

Last Ascension

The Conditioned

Eye Contact

Embraced

Unlawful (coming soon...)

The Outsiders

Love Beyond Time

Love Beyond Sanity

Love Beyond Loyalty

Love Beyond Sight

Love Beyond Expectations

Love Beyond Oceans

Love Beyond Flames

Love Beyond Lies (coming soon)

Cascade (completed series)

Haunted Redemption

Phoenix Everlasting

Fragility Unearthed

Persuasion Enraptured

Reverse Harem Story (completed series)

Unconventional

Unexpected

Undeniable

Kiss Her Goodbye

Hard Truths

Dark Truths

Deadly Truths (coming soon)

Shifter World

Planet Bear

Planet Wolf (coming soon)

Stand Alone Titles

Under The Lights

No Quitting Allowed

Mr. Wrong

Bite Marks

Bitten Surrender

The Vampire and The Virgin

Demon Within

Crimson Lust

Call Me Crazy (coming soon)

Writing with Ripley Proserpina

The Storm

Lightning Strikes

Thunder Rolling

The Deluge (coming soon)